First American Edition 2015
Kane Miller, A Division of EDC Publishing

Text Copyright © 2014 Nova Weetman
Illustration and Design Copyright © Hardie Grant Egmont 2014
First published in Australia by Hardie Grant Egmont 2014

For information contact:
Kane Miller, A Division of EDC Publishing
P.O. Box 470663
Tulsa, OK 74147-0663
www.kanemiller.com
www.edcpub.com
www.usbornebooksandmore.com

Library of Congress Control Number: 2014941180

Printed and bound in the United States of America
4 5 6 7 8 9 10
ISBN: 978-1-61067-354-9

Choose your own Ever After

A Hot Cold SUMMER

BY NOVA WEETMAN

Kane Miller
A DIVISION OF EDC PUBLISHING

Chapter One

"Mum! Have you seen my green bathing suit?" I yelled.

"No, honey. Sorry," she finally called back.

Urgh. I'd pulled out everything looking for it and now my room was a mess. I was always losing things. It didn't help that I lived between two houses – all my stuff went back and forth a lot.

Normally I just wore something else if I couldn't find what I was looking for, but I *needed* to find my green bathing suit. It was the last day of school before vacation and most of the kids in our class were meeting later at the pool, which meant one thing: it could be my last chance to hang with the gorgeous Tom Matthews.

If I wanted to see him during vacation, I'd have to arrange to meet up with him, or at least swap numbers. Either way, if it didn't happen this afternoon at the pool, then I wouldn't see him for the whole summer, and then my vacation would be totally boring. My best friend, Gen, was going away with her enormous family, both my parents were working, and almost everyone I knew had plans. I would have to spend six weeks hanging out on my own. Not cool. But if I could spend six weeks hanging out with Tom ...

"I did find this one, Frankie." My daydream was interrupted by Mum, who was now standing in the doorway to my room, holding up an old red bathing suit I hadn't worn since I'd quit the swim team. My face must have said it all because she looked at it and nodded. "Yes, it is a bit ..." She kind of lost her train of thought there. It was a thing she did. She was probably thinking about a work project.

"I can't wear that. It goes all baggy in the water. I *really* need my green one." I said, in a more whiney voice than I meant to use.

"Maybe you left it at your dad's," Mum tried.

As soon as she said it, I grinned. *Of course!* "Why didn't I think of that? Thanks, Mum!"

Luckily, my parents lived really close to each other and I could ride past Dad's on the way to school. I grabbed my schoolbag and bike helmet and headed to the front door.

"Have a good day, honey. I'll see you Sunday," said Mum, giving me a good-bye kiss.

I was back to thinking about Tom when I opened Dad's front door with my key. Distracted, I called out hello as I walked to my bedroom. I heard a door slam upstairs, but didn't think much of it.

"Dad, it's just me. I'm getting my bathing suit," I called out.

I had a quick look in my room, but I could see straightaway my suit wasn't there either. Then I remembered I'd gone to the pool one night with Gen and had rinsed off in the bathroom, leaving my bathing suit hanging over the shower curtain rod. I was always doing that, and Dad was always telling me to hang it out on the line.

As I started running up the stairs, Dad called out, "Frankie, can you wait a minute?"

I didn't stop, because I was already running late for school.

Dad lives in a neat little town house that he bought after he and Mum split up. It suits him perfectly, because everything has a place. And because he lives on his own, except for the nights I'm there, there's more than enough room. The only annoying thing is there's only one shower, in Dad's master bathroom, so he's forever telling me to hurry up when I'm in there. He doesn't seem to realize you can't rush a girl with wild, frizzy hair.

As I barged into the bathroom to search for my bathing suit, there was a scream. Shocked, I looked up and saw a woman wrapped in a towel staring at me with a horrified look on her face.

"Sorry, didn't mean to, um … who are you?" I

managed to say.

"I'm Jan," she answered, like I should have known.

"Oh. Okay. Ah, I just need my bathing suit," I said as I slipped past her to rifle through the laundry basket, where my things usually ended up when Dad found them in the bathroom.

"Do you mind?" She sounded a bit angry, which I guess was fair enough, but I didn't have time to be polite.

Dad had obviously heard the scream too, because suddenly he was squashing in behind me, forcing Jan and me even closer together.

"Frankie. Out, please," said Dad, using his stern voice.

Just then I saw the familiar green of my suit in the basket and snatched it out.

"See you later, Dad," I said as I squeezed around him and fought my way out of the bathroom.

But before I could make it down the stairs, Dad stopped me. I guess he wasn't expecting a visit from me this morning, so now he felt like he had to explain. I knew we'd have to talk about it, but I didn't really want to discuss it while Jan was still in his bathroom and could overhear.

"Frankie."

"Yeah, Dad."

"Um, that's Jan."

"Yeah, she told me." Was I supposed to know who Jan was?

"She's a friend," he said in a small voice. It was obviously really hard for him to have this conversation too. "A girlfriend. Um, my girlfriend," he continued. Then he looked surprised that he'd actually managed to say it.

"Great," I said – only because I couldn't possibly say what I was really thinking.

"We've been dating for a while now," said Dad as he suddenly found a spot of dirt on his shirt that needed attention. He was doing everything he could to avoid looking at me. And it might have been okay if Jan hadn't then come out of the bathroom, walked over to Dad and slid her arm through his like she was trying to show me they were a real couple. At least Dad managed to look as uncomfortable as I felt.

"Right, um, introductions. This is Jan. And this is Frankie," said Dad, with a bit of a wobble in his voice.

Jan and I stared at each other. It was weird looking at the first woman my dad had introduced me to since he and Mum had split. I knew he'd probably dated but he'd never been serious enough about anyone for me to meet them. And, to be honest, I'd sort of liked it that way.

"I've heard a lot about you, Frankie," Jan said with a smile.

"Great," I answered, sounding like it was the only word I knew. Why hadn't *I* heard about *her*? I just wanted to dig a big hole for myself and crawl in. "Well, nice to meet you, Jan," I said as I started to leave.

"I'll see you tonight, Frankie," she said.

"Tonight?" I asked, confused.

"Didn't your dad tell you?" she asked, looking between us. I didn't know what to say, because Dad hadn't told me anything.

Dad tried to catch my eye. "Er, Jan and I thought we'd all go out for dinner tonight."

Tonight. Now I understood. Tonight was my night with Dad. Two minutes ago I didn't even know Dad had a girlfriend. Now all of a sudden we were arranging to go out as a family, and apparently he was supposed to have told me already. I didn't want to be rude or upset Dad, but I wasn't going to pretend he'd told me something he hadn't.

Before I could say anything, Jan asked, "Is Thai okay?"

"Sure," I said, heading for the stairs. I just really wanted to get out of there.

I took the stairs faster than normal, and I'd almost made it to the front door when Dad said, "Just a sec."

"What?" I said, sounding really cross.

"I'm sorry. I should have told you," he said, looking me straight in the eye.

I nodded. "Yeah, you should have."

"And I meant to ask you about dinner. Do you mind? It *is* our night," he said.

I wanted to say, *Yeah, I mind*, but he looked really worried about what I was going to say and I'd never been very good at upsetting him. "It's fine."

"Only fine? Well, that doesn't sound good," he said, trying to win me with a smile.

"No more secrets. Okay?"

"Okay. Have a good last day! And don't get up to anything."

I rolled my eyes at him and he laughed. He was always saying things like that.

"Make sure you're home by seven. Jan made a reservation."

Skidding through the school gates, I slotted my bike into the rack. I didn't have time to bother with my massive lock. I was desperate to tell Gen about my dad, and if I didn't find her before school started I'd have to wait until lunch because we had different classes.

Gen wasn't at the lockers, so I chucked my bag in, grabbed my math book and hurried off to find her. But as I dashed around the corner to E building, I crashed straight into Tom. *The* Tom.

"Whoa, Frankie," he said, and grabbed my arm to stop me falling backward. I couldn't believe he was actually holding my arm.

"Sorry." I looked everywhere but at him.

"Whatevs," he said, as he let go of my arm and smiled at me. Like *right* at me. He had an amazing smile and I couldn't help but smile back. Those blue eyes. And that messy dark hair. As we stood there smiling at each other, I couldn't believe how cute he looked out of uniform for the last day, in his skinny black jeans and Ramones T-shirt.

"Are you guys coming to the pool today?" he asked.

I was so rapt he was asking if I was going, I didn't think. I just burst out with, "Oh yeah, I can't wait. I'm so hot!"

As Tom laughed, I realized what I'd just said. I could feel my cheeks blushing – it always happened when I said something embarrassing.

"Oh no, I didn't mean I'm *hot*," I tried to explain. "I just … well, it's really hot today."

He had a huge grin on his face, like he was enjoying

my embarrassment. "Yeah, sure," he said, infuriatingly. "Hey, I've been meaning to say that song you sang last week was awesome."

"Oh. Thanks," I said, trying to play it cool. I'd sung an original song at the school concert last week and people kept talking to me about it. But I didn't ever think Tom Matthews would be one of them. "Actually, it was pretty fun, getting up there," I admitted.

Then Tom really surprised me by saying, "We should get together and play. If you're around during vacation?"

"Sure," I managed, trying to stay cool. "That'd be great."

Was that actually his way of asking to hang out with me? Or did he just really like music?

"Well, see ya at the pool, Frankie," said Tom, as he walked off. Then he turned around and yelled, "Don't get too hot ..." with a giant smile on his face.

I watched him go. Even his back was cute. Now I just had to make sure we swapped numbers later. I couldn't wait to tell Gen that Tom and I were going to hang out and play music. How was I going to make it through a whole day of school? I just wanted to be at the pool with Tom. Now!

I survived math and found Gen waiting for me under the tree where we always had lunch. Gen had already scoffed down most of her sandwich. I'd have to eat mine quickly or she'd start on mine next. She was always super hungry because she had swimming practice most mornings. I didn't know why she didn't just bring two sandwiches of her own.

"Guess what?" I said as I slid down onto the grass next to her.

"You're finally allowed to get your ears pierced?"

I laughed. "As if." Both of us knew that wasn't going to happen until I was fourteen, which was still nearly a month away. My parents loved that they agreed on almost everything about what I *wasn't* allowed to do yet.

"So, spill," said Gen impatiently.

"Do you want the Dad news or the Tom news first?"

I said, trying to string it out.

She leaned closer, expecting something good. "Do you really have to ask?"

"Well, I crashed into Tom this morning and told him I was hot," I said, making her laugh. "And then he said we should hang out and play music during vacation."

"Ahhh!" squealed Gen. I looked around to make sure nobody could hear us. "You're going to make beautiful music together," she said, with a silly grin.

I rolled my eyes at her.

"Told you so," she said, with a huge grin on her face.

"Maybe. Maybe not. Maybe he was just being nice," I said, wanting reassurance.

"Of course he likes you. You're gorgeous. And lovely. And talented. And Tom Matthews would be lucky to go out with you."

"That's what I wanted to hear!" I said.

Gen had been telling me that Tom liked me for months. She believed she knew how boys really felt because she had three older brothers and she was always helping them with girls. I wanted to believe her. I really did, but after having my heart broken earlier in the year by a boy called Jack, I'd vowed to stay away from boys for a while. They were just too complicated.

"And, in other breaking news, Dad has a girlfriend," I said, surprised at how uncomfortable it made me just saying it. "Her name's Jan, and I walked in on her in the bathroom this morning."

"What? Oh no! Yuck! Was she naked?" she asked all in one breath.

I shook my head, smiling at the horrified look on Gen's face.

"But your dad doesn't have girlfriends! Since when?"

"I don't know. He didn't tell me about her. I just happened to find her in the bathroom, and now we're all having dinner tonight." I couldn't imagine sitting down at a table with Dad and Jan and watching them together, and feeling like I was in the way. I'd never felt like that with Dad before. We'd always gotten along really well.

"Frankie, that's awful. I can't believe he didn't tell you!" she said, leaning over to hug me.

"Me neither," I said, remembering how awkward it all was this morning.

Gen was the only friend I had who'd actually met my parents when they were still together, and she knew Dad hadn't had a girlfriend since the divorce eight years ago.

"There's something about parents dating when you aren't that makes it even worse. I guess if everything works out with Tom ..." she trailed off.

"*If* it works out?" I teased her.

"*When*. I meant *when* it works out," she said. "But don't you think? He's your dad and he's kissing someone. It's weird."

"I know. And she's nothing like Mum. That's weird too," I said, realizing I hadn't even considered that until now. But it was true. Mum was a career woman. She was tall and thin and always wearing something black and stylish. Jan was shorter and curvier and, when she'd finally gotten dressed, she was wearing old jeans and a T-shirt. In fact, they couldn't be more different.

"Does your mum know?" asked Gen, with a sort of panicked voice.

"I don't know," I said. I certainly wasn't going to tell her. Usually my parents were so good about all this stuff. They talked to each other and sorted things out so I didn't have to get in the middle, but Dad seemed to have kept Jan a secret.

"So are you okay about it?" asked Gen, as she stole the last part of my sandwich.

Was I? I didn't know. "I don't want him to be lonely, and it's not like I want Mum and Dad to get back together or anything ..." I started, then trailed off.

Gen finished my sentence for me. "But you don't really want to share your dad with someone you don't know. Right?"

"Exactly." I liked having Dad all to myself, and if he was already calling Jan his girlfriend then he was obviously pretty serious about her. Maybe all our time together would become about the three of us, and not just me and Dad.

"Hey, that's enough about your dad," said Gen standing up. "He's not going to ruin your day. Tell me more about Tom Who Thinks You're Hot."

I loved that Gen was so sure Tom liked me. I also loved that she thought everyone should love me. She was that kind of friend. But sometimes she was so blind about how great I was that she didn't actually read situations or people very well. So I couldn't always rely on her opinion. Still, she was right. Why let Dad having a girlfriend spoil the last day of school?

The rest of the afternoon sped by. We watched a movie in English class, because the fans had stopped working and it was too hot to do anything else. Mr. Phillips didn't even care when we all took our shoes off, and then he handed out popsicles and told us all to have a good vacation.

Some of the older kids were already having water fights as we walked through the school to our bikes. It was so hot that nobody actually cared if they got hit.

"Six whole weeks," said Gen, trying to eat the last of her popsicle before it dripped all over the ground.

"Hey, Gen, where's my bike?" I was sure I'd dropped it sort of near hers, but I couldn't see it anywhere.

"Where did you lock it?" asked Gen, looking around.

Then I remembered. "I didn't. I was running late." The thought hit me. "What if someone's stolen it?" I asked, worried about what her answer would be. I loved my bike. I rode it every day. I could get from my place to Gen's house in less than five minutes.

"It'll be here. Nobody would steal it," she said, trying to sound confident. "Kids leave their bikes unlocked all the time."

But as we searched the bike sheds, the fences, and all around the school, it was pretty clear that someone had taken it.

I felt sick. Dad had bought me that bike about five months ago and it was a really good one. Now I'd have to tell him that I hadn't even bothered locking it up.

Sensing I was close to tears, Gen hugged me.

"Maybe I should just head back to Dad's and break the news. You know, get it over and done with."

Before Gen could even answer me, Tom rode over with his friend Arlo.

"You guys coming to the pool?" asked Tom.

"My bike's been stolen," I said, feeling really stupid. I *always* locked my bike up. If only I hadn't been in such a rush to find Gen before school and tell her about Dad's new girlfriend.

"That sucks. You sure it's gone?" asked Tom.

"Yeah. I'm sure. It was right here," I said, pointing.

"We'll ride around school and see if we can find it. Someone might have just moved it," said Tom.

"We already checked," I said.

Tom shrugged. "That's okay, we'll look again."

As the boys rode off, I knew Gen was grinning at me.

"What?" I asked.

"He *likes* you," she said, laughing.

"Shhh, Gen. I don't want him to hear you!" I said, looking around.

I was pretty surprised that Tom had offered to search for my bike. I didn't really know him that well, except for sitting next to him in the school band rehearsals sometimes and being in science class together. Maybe Gen was right.

"Do you think Arlo's cute?" asked Gen.

I forgot about my bike for half a second. "You like him?" I asked, surprised.

She shrugged. "I don't know. I just don't want to be left out. If you're going to have a boyfriend ..." she said, smiling. "Then we could double-date! Unless you'd rather go out with your dad and his girlfriend."

I screwed up my face at that thought.

"Arlo's cute," I said to Gen.

I loved the idea of us all hanging out together. But before I could get too excited the boys reappeared on their bikes.

"Nothing," said Tom.

Oh. Dad was not going to be happy. He hated it when I just lost a book, or a hat. But my bike! That was a biggie.

"It might still turn up," said Gen hopefully, even though we both knew there probably wasn't much chance of that.

"Stu's bike was stolen last week," said Arlo. "They cut the lock."

That gave me a thought. Maybe I could pretend that somebody had cut through my lock. But that was a massive lie. I couldn't do that.

I'd have to tell my dad the truth. He was really big on me always being honest with him. But I'd probably have to do chores for a year before I'd get enough money for a new one. Then I'd never be able to buy my new guitar.

The boys were obviously waiting to see what we were going to do.

"So, are you coming to the pool?" asked Arlo.

I was pretty sure he was talking to Gen, and I was pretty sure she knew he was, because she didn't even wait for me to say anything. She just called out, "Yeah, we'll walk down. Meet you there."

Chapter Two

There were already heaps of kids in the water when we got to the pool, and we knew most of them. Last year was our first year of high school, but this year it really felt like we belonged.

We dumped all our stuff on the grass and looked around for Tom and Arlo.

"I can't see them, can you?" said Gen.

I felt a bit let down. I'd sort of expected they'd be waiting for us. But it *was* really hot. Maybe they were already in the water?

Gen and I used to do swim team together, but I stopped a couple of years ago. I hated getting up early three times a week to practice, but Gen loved it. I think she liked it because on those car trips to and from the pool, she got her mum all to herself. Gen didn't get a lot of alone time with her mum because she had such a big family.

Grinning at me, she raced me to the side, ignoring the "No Running" signs. We dived in together. The water was cool and perfect. It felt great, like summer was really starting.

"Can you see the boys?" I asked Gen when we surfaced. But she was too busy doing somersaults to even bother looking.

"Handstand competition?" asked Gen. We'd been doing handstands in the water since we first learned to swim.

"Okay. One, two, three," I said, and we both dived under.

Gen had only one hand on the bottom of the pool and she reached out for my hand with her other one. I went to hold it and we both tumbled out of our handstands. We surfaced again, laughing.

"Gen!" someone called out.

Gen turned to see who it was and was met with a face full of water.

It was Arlo. He ducked down in the water, escaping Gen's huge retaliatory splash. Then he resurfaced and splashed us again. And it was on.

For a minute I helped Gen get Arlo, and then I realized that Tom wasn't with him. I looked around but the pool was so busy I couldn't see him anywhere.

"Hey, Arlo, where's Tom?"

Arlo shot up out of the water, but he wasn't listening to me. He was too busy trying to dunk Gen.

"Arlo," I shouted this time.

This time Gen heard me. "Where's Tom?" she asked.

"On the grass," Arlo said, and then splashed Gen again. They seemed really comfortable with each other. I wished I could act that way with Tom.

I swam over to the edge and climbed out of the pool. There were kids everywhere. I wandered towards where I'd left my towel, but I was really looking for Tom.

I saw a boy lying on the grass. It looked like Tom from behind. I wrapped my towel around my waist and headed over.

Just as I reached him, a girl walked up with a can of soda. She sort of half smiled at me and then sat down on the grass next to where Tom was lying.

Maybe it wasn't him? I was about to go when the boy sat up and saw me. He smiled. It was that smile. And it *was* that Tom.

"Oh hey, Frankie, you made it," he said.

"Yeah," I said, wondering who the girl was. She didn't go to our school, and I hadn't seen her around.

Then she opened the can, took a sip and handed it to Tom.

"Thanks, Jas," he said softly and then looked at me again. "This is Frankie. She's the one I told you about."

The girl nodded and smiled at me. "You're the singer?"

"Yeah," I said, feeling confused.

"Oh, sorry, this is Jasmine. My girlfriend. She sings too and I thought it would be great to get you guys together."

"Tom said your song was amazing," said Jasmine. "I'd love to hear it."

Oh. *He did like me, but only because I could sing.*

"Do you want to sit down?" asked Tom. "We should swap numbers so we can get together during vacation."

I couldn't believe I'd gotten it so wrong. He was just being friendly. As if I wanted to get together with him and his *girlfriend*.

"Yeah, sure. But I'm just going to go and grab a drink," I said, desperate to get away from them.

"Cool," said Tom as he smiled at me, obviously not understanding that any of this was a big deal. At least he had absolutely no idea that *I* liked *him*.

I walked straight back to the pool and looked around for Gen. She was still splashing water at Arlo. I jumped in and swam over to her.

"Did you find him?" asked Gen, ducking away from Arlo.

I nodded. "He's with his girlfriend."

Gen made a face. "No. What? But that can't be right!"

I shrugged. "It is. Her name's Jas."

"Oh, Frank. I'm sorry. I really thought …" and she wrapped her arms around me, pulling me in for a hug.

"I'm just going to go home," I said, hoping she'd get out of the pool and come with me.

But instead she said, "Do you want me to come?"

Of course I did. Gen was my best friend. I felt sad and embarrassed and like I kept getting in the way of other people's relationships. But I didn't want to *make* her come. I wanted her to insist.

Before I could even tell her I wanted her to leave with me, Arlo burst out of the water behind us, and dragged Gen under, dunking her. She came up laughing and turned around to get him back. Obviously I had an answer – she was having way too much fun to leave with me.

Trying not to be hurt, I climbed out of the pool, pulled on my clothes over my wet bathing suit, and started walking towards the exit. I'd almost made it, when Gen grabbed my arm.

"Frankie, where are you going?"

"Home. It's fine. You can stay," I said, trying to smile.

"Really? You won't be cross later?" she asked, knowing me too well.

"Probably," I said.

"If you want me to come with you …" she said.

For some reason I just couldn't tell her I wanted her to come with me. Maybe it was because people had sort of disappointed me all day, and I just wanted my best friend to *know* when I needed her. Instead I smiled weakly and said good-bye, and then I walked through the turnstiles and left.

I was playing guitar in my bathing suit when Mum came home. I wasn't supposed to still be at her house, but I'd come back to grab my stuff for Dad's, and I just hadn't gotten very far. Sometimes if things were pretty crappy, I'd sit on my bed and play my guitar for ages. It usually made me feel better but, strangely, it wasn't working tonight. I kept seeing the look on Tom's face when he innocently introduced me to his girlfriend.

"Honey? Why aren't you at your dad's?" she asked as she walked into my bedroom and leaned down to give me a kiss. I guess the sound of the guitar was a bit of a giveaway that I was here. "Are you okay?" she asked.

"Yeah," I said, then added, "actually, not really."

Mum sat down next to me on the bed. "Did something happen at school?"

I didn't know where to start. I didn't usually tell her about boys and I wasn't ready to start now. And I couldn't talk about Dad, and I didn't know what to say about Gen. There was only one thing that I really could talk about and I felt guilty saying it.

"Um, my bike got stolen," I said.

"How? Don't you have that giant lock?" she asked.

I was wondering what to say, when she said, "You did lock it, didn't you?" Sometimes it seemed Mum could almost read my mind.

"Um, nope, I didn't," I said, and felt relieved that I hadn't tried to lie my way out.

"Oh, honey," she said in *that* voice, which I knew meant she was really disappointed in me.

"Please, don't say anything else. I know. It's been a bad day. I'll pay for a new bike somehow. And I know I have to tell Dad," I said, before she could add anything.

"Well, okay. We can talk about it later," she said. "Actually, Frankie, I had something to ask you." She looked serious. "I found out today that Tony can't go to London to collect the international design award we won, because his wife's sick. As associate architect, I'm going to have to go."

I looked up. "Oh? Well, that's good, isn't it?" I said.

"Well, yes, but it's next week, so it's a bit quick. I have to leave on Thursday. And I'd be away for two weeks."

"Does Dad know I'll be staying with him?" I said, hoping he wasn't too unhappy at the thought of having me around now that he was dating.

"Yes, and of course he's happy to have you. But here's the thing, Frankie: I can take someone with me." I wondered if she was about to tell me she had a new boyfriend hiding in the cupboard that I didn't know about, but instead, she smiled and said, "And you've never been to London."

I sat up quickly. "What?" I said, wondering if what I thought she'd just said was true.

She nodded. "Do you want to come?"

Okay. Stop there, forget about my bad day. London?

"Yes! That'd be awesome," I said, trying to get my head around the idea of going to London in a week.

"I would have to do some work from the London office. And instead of staying in a hotel, I thought it might be fun to stay at Tina's," Mum went on.

That stopped my enthusiasm. "As in Tina and *Jack*?" I asked, already knowing the answer. Tina was my mum's best friend. Her son Jack was my age and when he and Tina had stayed with us earlier in the year, I'd had a pretty massive crush on him.

But Mum obviously didn't hear the concern in my voice because she smiled as she said, "Wouldn't it be good to see Jack again?"

I managed to nod, because I didn't trust myself to say anything. I really wasn't sure how I felt about seeing Jack again. I had thought we could be friends, but the way he'd cut off all contact with me and just stopped answering my e-mails had been horrible.

"Well, anyway, have a think and let me know tonight. If you do want to come we have to get organized." She laughed as she looked around my garbage dump of a room. "And that's not really our strong point is it, Frankie?"

Walking to Dad's, I couldn't stop thinking about going to London. I'd never been overseas before, and it would be an amazing place for a vacation. But it had been ages since I'd seen Jack, and I'd just managed to stop thinking about him. Did I really want to go through all that again?

As I got to Dad's, I heard my phone go. I knew it was Gen. She'd already left a bunch of messages. I didn't want to talk to her but if I didn't answer it now, she'd just keep calling until I did.

She started talking as soon as I answered. "I'm sorry, Frankie. I should have come with you," she said.

"That's okay," I said, not really meaning it.

"Don't do that. Please. You always do that. It makes me feel even worse," she said.

"Okay. You should have come with me. I would have come with you," I said, feeling angry enough to spill exactly how I felt.

I could hear her breathing but not saying anything.

"No, you wouldn't," she said finally. "When Jack was here you let me go home on my own from Sam's party."

I couldn't believe she'd stored that up. I was about to argue, when I realized she was right. But still, it didn't make me feel any better.

She must have sensed I was still hurt, because she said, "I'm sorry, okay? I wanted to hang out with Arlo."

I couldn't believe how honest she was sometimes. I loved that she could just blurt out whatever it was she felt, even though it meant I'd be hurt because I was the one she was blurting it at.

"Since when do you like him? You didn't say anything," I said, realizing that half of my hurt came from the fact that she'd kept it hidden. I'd been going on about Tom for months and she'd never mentioned Arlo.

"It's no big deal, Frank. He's nice. He's cute. I like him. We had fun. That's all. I'm not like you about boys," she said. "I don't really think about them unless they're around."

I started laughing. I just couldn't help myself. "Liar. What about that Charlie whatshisname? And Marcus?"

She started laughing too. "All right. I'm not *quite* as bad as you," she said. "But yeah, I should have come home with you. But then you should have asked me to come. So we're both crap. Okay?"

That was the thing about Gen. No matter how much we argued we always sorted it out really quickly, because she wouldn't let it go. Even when I refused to answer my phone or I was sulking or whatever, she'd just keep at me until it was okay again.

By the time I got off the phone, I felt much better. Even though I'd hoped to be the one having fun with a boy at the pool, I was really happy for my best friend. And I realized I'd forgotten to tell her about London.

Maybe I just didn't want her to tell me not to go. She'd been the one to deal with the Jack fallout and I knew what she'd say if I told her I was going to be staying with him for two weeks. I wasn't in a hurry for that conversation.

Dad had arranged to meet Jan at the restaurant, because I think he wanted to have a bit of time just with me beforehand.

"So are you really cross with me?" he asked, as we were walking down the main street to the restaurant.

"Um, I'm not exactly cross. But I'm hurt. And I wish you'd told me about Jan."

"Sorry, Frankie. I just didn't know how to tell you. I think I was a bit embarrassed about saying I had a girlfriend. At my age. It's sort of funny, isn't it?"

Hilarious. It just seems like everyone has girlfriends. Or boyfriends. Except me.

"Anyway, I'm glad you found out, because I want

you two to get to know each other," he said.

Then he told me he'd had coffee with Mum to tell her about Jan because he didn't want me to have to keep it a secret.

"And your mum told me about London," he said.

It had sort of been a day where I misread people, so I decided just to ask straight out. "Do you want me to go?" I asked, feeling a bit prickly. "So you and Jan can have a few weeks without me around?"

Dad started laughing. "No. I don't want you to go. In fact, I've been looking forward to spending time with you this vacation. I've taken a couple of weeks off and Jan has a beach house on the coast. There's plenty of room. That's what Jan was going to ask you tonight. I know you love the beach."

I stopped walking and looked at Dad, not sure that I understood him correctly. "She was going to ask me to come on vacation with you? Both of you?"

He nodded. "Yes. You can even learn to surf if you like. I know you've always wanted to."

I was so pleased that Dad still wanted me around

that I surprised us both and threw my arms around his neck, hugging him way too tight.

"Is that a yes?" he said, laughing.

As I let go of him, I realized how lucky I was. My parents had both invited me on fantastic trips. Now all I had to do was decide which one. London would be so cool, but it would be hard to see Jack again after he'd hurt me. And I really loved the beach, but I wasn't sure how I felt about hanging out with Dad's new girlfriend.

This was going to be harder than I thought.

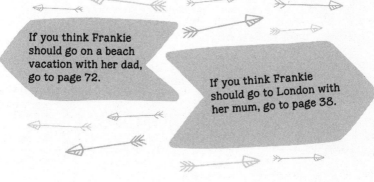

If you think Frankie should go on a beach vacation with her dad, go to page 72.

If you think Frankie should go to London with her mum, go to page 38.

Frankie GOES TO LONDON WITH her *mum*

Chapter Three

I couldn't believe I was about to see Jack again. Did he still have that shaggy hair that fell down over his eyes, and the skinny jeans with the ripped knee?

Ever since I'd decided to go to London with Mum, I couldn't stop thinking about him. Gen had made a pact with me that I could go to London and stay with Jack and have a great vacation, if – and only if – I did not fall for him again. We could be friends. Just friends.

It's just that usually I didn't get this nervous on the way to seeing one of my "friends."

I knew Gen was right, especially after the way he'd treated me, but I just couldn't help it. I was in

London! And about to see a boy I had once really liked. Although my stomach turned into knots when I started wondering how *he* felt about *me*.

I hadn't thought about him much on the plane because I'd watched about ten movies to try to make the flight go faster. And now that we were actually here and I was staring out the window of Tina's car, I felt like I was in one of those films, just watching London flick by.

Something big and red drove past us. "Is that a double-decker bus?" I asked.

Mum and Tina both laughed from the front of the car. "Yep. Thought we'd take the scenic way home. Just so you could get an idea of London," said Tina.

I was too excited to answer her. I couldn't believe I was finally seeing all the sights. "Westminster Abbey?" I asked, staring out the back window. "And Big Ben?"

"How do you know so much about London, Frankie?" asked Tina as she stopped at the blinking traffic lights.

"Google," I said, half truthfully. When Jack came to Australia he'd stayed with us for nearly a month, and after he'd left, I spent a lot of time researching because I wanted to know more about where he came from and what it was like.

Mum and Tina obviously had no idea how much I'd liked Jack then so I wasn't about to admit that now.

Then Tina piped up from the front. "I think Jack's planning on showing you around."

"Oh. Great," I said. The thought made my heart race. "But he doesn't have to. I'm sure he's pretty busy." I hoped my pact would hold after I'd actually seen him. It was one thing promising Gen I could just be friends while he was still on the other side of the world but it was totally different when I was staying in the same house as him.

"Never too busy for you, Frankie!" Tina answered and smiled in the rearview mirror at me.

I tried to smile back but the truth was I still didn't know how I felt about seeing Jack again. We'd had such an awesome time together before – so part of me was hoping it would be like that again. But the way he'd just stopped e-mailing me back without telling me why made me wary of getting too close.

"This is the main street," Tina was saying. "And that's where you catch a bus into town." She pointed out a stop. "There're lots of good places along here to buy clothes, too," she said, more to Mum than me.

Although I was planning on doing lots of shopping while I was here, I wanted to check out the big-city stores rather than the little boutiques on the local main street. Actually, I didn't have much money to spend, especially after I'd forked out a lot of my savings from busking on a new bike, but Gen and I had researched the cool shops to go to, and she'd written a list of things she wanted me to look out for. We'd joked that I was going to have to buy an extra bag to get it all home.

As we drove, I stared out the window, taking in all that I could. It was so different from what I was used to. Lots of the buildings looked really old and even though the sun hadn't come up completely yet, there were people everywhere.

"So this is our street ..." Tina turned off the main street and into a more suburban-looking area. "And this is home," she said, pulling up outside a beautiful old two-story house.

It was exactly like the house I'd imagined. Skinny and tall just like Jack. *Friends*, I said quietly to myself. *Just friends.*

"Come on, Frankie. Let's go see if that boy is up," said Tina, as she led us up the steps.

I really hoped he wasn't, so I could have a shower and get changed before I saw him, but as we stepped inside, we were greeted by the smell of bacon and eggs, and loud music blaring from the kitchen, which meant only one thing: he was up.

I felt quite nervous as we walked through the house towards the music. I'm not sure if it was the jet lag or the expectation of coming face-to-face with Jack, but I was feeling all churned up. We stepped into the kitchen. Jack spun around with a sizzling frying pan, and I felt my heart lurch.

He grinned. "Welcome to London, ladies! Hungry? I've done a fry-up."

His hair was all wild and crazy like he'd just rolled

out of bed. But it didn't matter, because he still looked gorgeous: the same scruffy brown hair, big brown eyes and perfect smile I'd remembered. But he was even cuter than I'd thought. How was I going to stop myself falling for him all over again?

"Frankie? Do you still love crispy bacon?" he asked as he piled it high with some thick white toast.

"Um, I'm not really that hungry, thanks," I said, even though I was starving. The plane food had been fairly ordinary and crispy bacon was pretty much my favorite thing in the world. I was rapt that he'd remembered, but I didn't want to have to make small talk while we all ate together, at least not until I'd had some sleep, brushed my teeth and worked out the whole time zone thing.

But before I could escape, Tina maneuvered me into a chair, handed me some cutlery and the plate.

"Put something in your stomach," said Tina. "And don't be deceived by Jack, this is the only thing he can cook. He's just showing off."

"Mum. Don't give away my secrets," said Jack, smiling at me.

I wondered what other secrets he had – and if I'd get to know any of them while I was here.

When Jack sat down next to me his leg bumped against mine and for a second everything stopped. I remembered how it felt the last time we'd seen each other.

I must have looked a bit out of sorts because Mum leaned over and asked, "You tired, honey?"

"No," I said, yawning.

Tina laughed. "Frankie, why don't you go up and have a little sleep. When you wake up we can go and do something."

I nodded, realizing I was totally exhausted. Suddenly the only thing I wanted to do was sleep.

As I got up to follow Tina upstairs, Jack looked up at me. "If you're not going to eat that ..." he said, gesturing at my unfinished breakfast.

Before I could answer he snatched the bacon off my plate with a grin, and I couldn't stop myself grinning back. Gen would have been horrified. She'd made me promise that no matter how cute he was, I wouldn't be too friendly. And here I was, already grinning at him within ten minutes of arriving.

Jack jumped up. "You eat, Mum, I'll show Frankie upstairs."

"No, it's fine. I'll find it myself," I tried to insist. But Jack grabbed me by the arm and pretty much pulled me from the kitchen.

Having him so close made my heart race, and I was so busy trying not to check him out from behind as he led me to the stairs that I didn't hear a word he was saying.

He must have realized I wasn't listening, because he stopped at the top of the stairs and looked at me strangely. "Frankie? Did you hear me?"

"What? Oh, sorry. I wasn't really listening."

"Really? I have to say it again? I was just saying sorry for not e-mailing you back. I just figured that, well, you know."

But I didn't know. I had no idea how *he* felt about it. All I knew was that kissing him was the only thing I'd thought about for months after he left. We'd had an awesome month together, and then, on the night before he was due to go back to London, we'd kissed.

For the eight months since then, I'd been hung up on him, even though he lived on the other side of the world and wasn't even in touch with me most of that time. We'd e-mailed for a while, but we kept it friendly and never really talked about the kiss. And then, one day, he'd stopped e-mailing. Just like that. I couldn't work out what had happened. Even Gen got bored listening to me talk about him, and that's saying something. No wonder she'd been so encouraging about Tom Matthews.

"Anyway, Frankie, I didn't mean to just vanish," he said as he shuffled awkwardly around. Obviously it was really hard for him to say it.

I really wanted to know what had happened. But before I could work out how to phrase it, my mouth yawned.

Jack frowned. "Am I boring you?"

"No. I'm sorry. I'm just really tired," I said, feeling my eyes closing.

"Yeah, course. Anyway, I'm really glad you're here.

We're going to have some serious fun, Frankie," he said, and then leaned down and gave me a hug.

My whole body went sort of stiff as he pulled me close. I could smell his sweater and feel how strong his arms were around me. As unexpected as it was, I could've stood there all day, just being wrapped up in Jack's hug. It took me back to that night when it seemed like we were made for each other.

He let me go and smiled. "I like your hair like that."

He liked my hair? Huh? I'd just been on a plane for two days. Maybe Gen was right. Maybe I shouldn't have come. I'd only been in London for a few hours and now I was wondering how I could keep my hair exactly the same for the next two weeks.

"I really want us to be good friends," he said as he showed me to the room I was going to share with Mum.

"Yep. Me too," I said. *What a liar!* Of course I didn't want that. I had heaps of friends. I didn't need another one.

"Have a good sleep," he said, and shut the door to my room.

It's pretty hard to sleep when the smile of a cute boy keeps popping into your head. It was like a little promise of something to come. As much as I tried to pretend I didn't still like him, I couldn't help hoping that maybe we would have a great time together while I was here. Maybe we would find some of the closeness we had in Australia. And maybe, this time, he wouldn't break my heart.

I woke up to the sound of a guitar playing. At first I was really disoriented. The room was dark and I was still in my clothes. Then I remembered where I was: London.

It was *Jack* playing guitar.

I really wanted to see him, but I also wanted to look better than I had after getting off the plane.

I found the bathroom and looked at the unfamiliar shower fixture, shivering as I worked out which dial to use. I finally got in, scrubbed away at my jet-lagged body with some of Tina's fancy shower gel, and started feeling human again.

Back in my bedroom, I pulled everything out of my suitcase, looking for my jeans and my favorite red sweater, and started trying to fix my hair. Then I remembered that Jack liked it crazy and I stopped and messed up the front again so it looked more like it did when I'd arrived.

As I walked into the family room, Jack was sitting on the floor with his guitar on his knee, strumming.

It made me think about all the nights back in Australia when we'd stayed up after Mum and Tina had gone to bed, playing our guitars softly so we wouldn't wake them.

It was on the last one of those nights that we'd kissed.

I must have leaned against the door because it creaked, and Jack looked around. I expected him to be embarrassed that I'd been watching him, but he just smiled.

"Finally. I've been waiting all day for you to wake up."

"Really? All day? So that's why I'm starving," I said.

"Well, you'll have to wait. The Mums have gone out somewhere for a few hours and when they get back we're going to an Indian place up the road."

He'd always called them The Mums. I liked it, because it made it seem there was *us* and there was *them*. I realized this meant we had the house all to ourselves. I tried not to think about that.

He patted the floor. "Come on. We still have time for a few songs."

When I'd met Jack, I was playing guitar in the school band, and only ever singing privately in my room. One day he overheard me and got so excited he made me realize I could sing and write songs. Now there was nothing I loved more.

I sat down on the floor near him, but not too close. "New guitar?" I asked, noticing the different wood and shape.

"Yeah. It was Dad's. My uncle had been looking after it since Dad died and he gave it to me last month. It's a beauty," he said, touching the strings. "I like that Dad used to play it. It makes it even more special."

And it was. It was the sort of guitar I'd buy if I had the money.

"Can I play it?" I asked, not sure if he'd mind.

He grinned cheekily at me. "Only if you sing 'Tomorrow Land' with me first."

I rolled my eyes at him. "Nah."

"Oh, come on."

It was a song I wrote when Jack was staying with us, and I hadn't sung it since, because it reminded me of being with him. I didn't want to sing it now, especially with him sitting so close.

"Pleeeeaaase," he begged.

"I've forgotten how it goes," I lied.

"Lucky I haven't, then," he said and started strumming it on his guitar. "Join in, Frank."

Other than Gen, he was the only person who ever called me that, and it was strange how much I liked hearing him say it.

As he hit the chorus, he looked over at me as if to say, *Come on*. I loved hearing him play. And I was amazed he remembered how the song went.

I wanted to sing. We used to have so much fun jamming together – and it was my song, after all. But I wasn't expecting we'd be like this again so quickly. I'd thought it would be strange for a while. I thought I'd be angry with him for how much he'd hurt me.

But I just couldn't help myself. I loved the chorus too much not to join in.

"In my tomorrow land

when you take my hand

and open up the sky

so that we can flyyyyy."

I hit the last note in perfect time with Jack. He gave a sharp nod, and we both stopped together. He laughed, and in that moment, it was like things were exactly as they used to be between us.

"That was awesome!" he said. "You have to sing it tomorrow night."

I looked at him, confused. "Tomorrow night?"

Jack put his guitar down on the couch. "Our band's doing a gig at a record store tomorrow night. They have this stage in the back where bands can play."

"Cool," I said, impressed. But it made me realize things had really changed.

He nodded. "Well, hopefully. We haven't had much time to practice lately. But if we do well, we might get a residency. It's our first real gig."

"I didn't know you had a band," I said, feeling sad that there were now obviously so many things I didn't know about his life.

"It's a bunch of friends from school. I play guitar and write most of the songs. Will you come? And sing?" he asked, sounding excited.

"Okay," I said, without thinking it through.

Before Jack could say anything, someone called out, "Jack, who's singing?"

I looked up to see a girl standing in the doorway. She was wearing a short denim skirt, big boots and a striped sweater. She was probably about my age but she was wearing red lipstick and had her blonde hair cut short, which made her look older. And pretty cool.

She walked over to where we were sitting on the floor.

Jack smiled up at her as she came closer. "Asha, meet Frankie."

"Oh, so *you're* Frankie," said Asha, barely looking at me.

Great. This was feeling all too familiar. First Dad and Jan. Then Tom and Jasmine. Now Jack and Asha. Was she his girlfriend or just some random girl who had a key to his mum's house? And why had she heard about me when I hadn't heard about her?

"Yeah, I'm Frankie," I said, feeling a bit defensive.

"I'm Jack's girlfriend. And the singer in the band," she said, sitting down so close to Jack her leg was resting on his.

Girlfriend. I tried to hide how I felt about hearing that fantastic bit of news.

Jack gave me a sort of half smile, like he was sorry he hadn't mentioned it before. Then he turned to Asha and said, "Hey, don't you think it's a great idea? Frankie can sing 'Tomorrow Land' at the gig."

She frowned at him. "Is that that song you're always playing?"

Jack's cheeks flushed a little. "Yeah. It's a great song," he said. "I think we should definitely play it tomorrow."

"Is it your song?" she asked me.

I nodded. "Yeah." Maybe I should have added, *It was the song I wrote for your boyfriend and I'd almost gotten it out of my head until he stirred it all up again.*

Asha reached her arms around Jack and pulled him in close. Was it my imagination or did he look a bit awkward?

"Well, really, the only thing that matters is what you think, Frankie," said Asha. I wasn't sure if she was asking me what I thought of her being Jack's girlfriend, or how I felt about singing, so I avoided the question altogether.

"I think I want to have a turn on your guitar, Jack. Wasn't that the deal?"

Jack passed it to me. "All yours."

I moved up onto the couch, wanting to get away from them. I wish I'd known he had a girlfriend. At least I could have been better prepared.

The guitar was lighter than I'd expected and it tucked into my body like a good guitar should. I strummed a few chords and the sound was amazing.

"Wow," I said, as my fingers worked the strings.

Jack joined me on the couch. "I know, right? It's perfect," he said, excited. "It just makes everything sound so much better."

Asha was obviously feeling left out because she piped up with, "I thought *we* were supposed to be practicing tonight, Jack."

Jack groaned. "Oh, sorry, Ash. We're going out for Indian."

I was surprised he'd chosen to have dinner with Mum and me over his girlfriend. She was obviously surprised too because she shot him an angry look and said, "I thought this gig was important to you."

"Yeah, it is. Of course," he said as he took the guitar from me. "But –"

"You'll just have to miss dinner. We can get something later." She smiled at me like she'd won.

I waited for Jack to make a decision. I really hoped he'd tell her he was coming with us. Instead he shrugged at me, like he had no choice.

"Can you apologize to The Mums for me," he asked, with a guilty smile. "Next time, Frank."

"Sure," I said, forcing a smile. "Next time." I wasn't about to show either of them how disappointed I was. It wasn't just that he had a girlfriend. It was that he'd chosen someone like Asha over me.

Dinner was a disaster. I only managed half a samosa, and Mum kept asking me if I was okay. She even leaned across at one point and checked to see if I was feeling hot.

Tina basically ordered half the menu, but after meeting Asha I just wasn't hungry anymore. In the end I managed to pass it off as jet lag and Tina brought four boxes of leftover food home for Jack to eat whenever he showed up.

Because I'd slept all day, I was wide awake. So, while Mum snored on the bed next to me, I started writing a super-long message to Gen. Before I could press send, she sent me one. It was always like that with us. We had this thing where we'd think about each other at exactly the same time.

She wanted to know about Jack and I told her he had a girlfriend. She sent three smiley faces at that bit of news with a message telling me she was glad because it meant I wouldn't go falling for him all over again.

Technically, she was right.

But I couldn't help feeling that there was still something between us. When we'd played music together tonight, it felt just like it did on the night we kissed.

Having a girlfriend didn't mean he couldn't still like me. It just meant that he wouldn't do anything about it. And now I'd never know for sure how he felt about me.

I had liked him – a lot. And I really wanted to believe he'd felt the same way about me.

Mum dragged me out of bed to go shopping with her and Tina. Given that I'd only managed to get to sleep as she was getting up, I was pretty cranky about it. Perhaps if they'd only wanted to go to a couple of shops it might have been okay, but they went into every single middle-aged-lady shop on the street. After suffering through nearly three hours of this, I finally begged off and told them I'd meet them at home.

Suddenly I was on my own. In London. I could do whatever I liked. And I'd just spotted a record store on the other side of the road.

One of my favorite things, apart from actually playing music or listening to music, was looking for music. And old vinyl was the bomb.

Dad gave me his old record player years ago and ever since I've had it hooked up to some speakers so I could play whatever I liked in my room.

That was the other thing about Jack staying with us: we had spent hours listening to music. All sorts of stuff. Jazz and rock, punk and pop. Most kids I knew had an iPod and they listened to the top twenty or they watched music videos on YouTube, but I was a sucker for the old stuff.

As soon as I walked into the record store, I was in heaven. The shop was huge inside; there was awesome music pumping through the speakers. There were hundreds of crates full of vinyl and heaps of people just standing there, flicking through the records.

I found a box and started looking. There was a mix of stuff I'd never heard of before, stuff I knew, and stuff I desperately wanted. I had a limited budget so it took me a while to make a decision about what to get, but I walked up to the counter feeling pretty pleased with my first purchase in pounds sterling.

At the counter, I looked up and noticed a massive sign: TONIGHT @ 7PM: THE ANGRY DUCKS
Jack's band!

I looked around again. There *was* a stage right at the back, where it looked like bands could play.

I couldn't believe they were going to be playing here, and that I had a chance to get up on stage here too. I handed over my money and stepped out onto the street, feeling that whatever happened – or didn't happen – with Jack, London was going to be fun.

Even though the house was within walking distance of the main street, I couldn't resist the idea of catching a red bus home. Tina had warned me the bus route was not exactly direct, but I felt like sitting on the upper deck and watching the world go by. I was headed towards the bus stop when I saw a dress hanging in the window of a shop. I'm not a dress girl. But *this* dress was talking to me. In fact, it really seemed to be waving its gorgeous long black sleeves in my direction.

I *had* to go in and try it on.

The dress was different from anything else I owned, so I wasn't sure if it would suit me. Usually I shopped with Gen – and I knew she'd never let me buy anything really shocking. But now I had to decide by myself. It wasn't that I struggled with what to wear all the time, just when it was something like buying a black dress. If it were a new pair of shorts, I'd have no trouble deciding.

I came out of the dressing room to look in the mirror.

It was weird how a dress that had looked so good on the rack could look so awful on me. I started tugging at it, trying to fix it, but it was still all wrong.

I was about to give up when the shop assistant appeared.

"Do you mind if I just …?" she said, and started

rearranging the fabric. "Now look."

"Wow!" I said.

"Yep. I know, right? Amazing." She smiled.

And, weirdly, it was. I suddenly looked older and more confident. I never knew a dress could make me look so good. If Jack still wanted me to sing "Tomorrow Land" at his gig, then this was the perfect dress.

"And it's on sale," the shop assistant said.

"Okay. I'll take it," I said, hoping I had enough money left.

"You probably need some heels with that dress."

Heels? I never wore heels. I couldn't even walk in heels. Before I could answer, she held up a little black boot with a heel.

"Cute, don't you think?"

It was. I would love to wear something like that, but I'd probably break both my ankles if I tried.

"They are almost made for that dress," she said, with just the right amount of knowing.

"It's fine. I've got shoes already," I said, my ankles thanking me.

It was raining when I walked out of the shop. The kind of fine misty rain that somehow causes frizzy, curly hair like mine to transform into a giant puff ball. So I ran to the bus shelter. As I waited for the bus, I saw Jack and Asha on the other side of the road. They seemed to be arguing.

Then a bus pulled up and I climbed on. As it pulled away, I felt bad for hoping that their fight might've had something to do with me.

"Frankie Jones!" said Mum that night. "You look about seventeen."

I waited. Was she going to tell me to get changed?

"Amazing!" she said, as she reached forward and gave me a hug. "You look amazing."

"Really?" I asked, a bit surprised at Mum's enthusiasm.

"Really. Money well spent. Are you trying to impress anyone in particular?" she asked in an offhand way, which I knew was her way of asking me if I liked Jack.

"Just you. And Tina."

She smiled. "Well, it worked. Now let's get going or they'll have finished playing by the time we arrive."

"Are you two happy to walk?" asked Tina.

I made a face. "Really? It's raining. And freezing."

She laughed. "And the easiest way to get there."

"Okay, okay. I'll walk in the freezing cold snow!" I said dramatically.

"Frankie! It's not snowing," she said.

"There's still time," I said as we stepped outside into the icy night air.

When we walked into the record store and made our way towards the stage, I saw that most of the chairs were already taken and lots of people were standing. My heart pounded. I didn't know if I was nervous for Jack, nervous about seeing him, or nervous about singing.

Tina stopped to talk to people, so Mum and I found a spot near the front. We always stood down at the front when we went to see bands. Mum liked live music almost as much as I did, and luckily she didn't mind taking me with her. It meant I got to see lots of bands, although she usually made me wear earplugs!

"You made it," said Jack as he walked up.

"Of course," I said, taking off my giant puffer jacket. As I hung it over the back of a chair, I noticed Jack was looking at me.

"You look great," he said, sounding almost surprised.

I shrugged, like it was nothing special, but inside I was super happy he'd noticed.

"Are you still okay to sing?" he asked. "We can do it as the last song. You'd be our special overseas guest," he added with a smile.

I'd probably never get another chance to sing in London with Jack's band. And it would be pretty cool performing where nobody knew me.

"Yeah, okay," I said, secretly more than a little excited about getting on stage.

Jack grinned at me, and then the lights dimmed. "Better go, this is us," he said, and rushed off.

As I watched him disappear into the crowd, I wondered if he felt like I did whenever I performed. Sort of sick beforehand and then, as soon as it started, totally pumped.

The spotlight came on, and Asha walked onto the stage, stopping at the microphone. I looked her up and down. And I couldn't believe it: she was wearing the same dress as me. Along with the cute little black boots from the shop. I might have looked better than I normally did, but *she* looked like a rock star.

I *couldn't* go on stage now. It would be totally embarrassing. Wouldn't it?

Then the spotlight hit Jack. He brushed his hair out of his eyes. "A one, a two, a one, two, three, four."

I'd never seen him on stage before. We'd always just jammed at home. But he was incredible. Electric. Once he started playing I didn't look at anyone else. Just him.

Even if I hadn't known he'd written the songs, I would have loved them. They were more upbeat pop songs than I'd expected, and people started dancing. Even Mum.

The whole band was tight and slick, like they'd played together for years. Asha had a great, gravelly voice; it really suited the lyrics. It was weird, though, watching the two of them on stage together. They didn't seem very couple-y. Or maybe I was just hoping.

They sang about twenty songs and then Asha called out, "Thanks for coming, everyone, we're the Angry Ducks, and you've been great!"

The crowd cheered and people started calling out for more. I watched Jack say something to Asha, who shook her head before walking off the stage. I knew Jack was about to call me up and I wasn't sure what to do. I didn't want to wear the same dress as Asha on stage, but I really wanted to sing.

Then Jack grabbed the microphone. "We've sung all *our* songs, sorry. Next time we'll write a few extras." People in the audience laughed. "But I have a friend in the audience all the way from Australia and she's going to sing a special song for you tonight. Please make her welcome – Frankie Jones!"

Mum and Tina smiled at me, pushing me forward. I hesitated, and Mum must have sensed I was feeling funny about it, because she leaned forward and said, "Go on, honey."

"I'm wearing the same dress as Asha," I whispered.

She shrugged. "Nobody will notice."

Of course, she was right. What was I worried about? Asha wasn't even on stage. I reached my hand up to Jack and he pulled me up. I'm sure he held my hand for a second longer than he needed to, but it felt so perfect that I didn't care.

"Let's smash it, Frank," he said into my ear, sending a tingle down my spine.

I walked up to the microphone and lowered it. Then I took a big breath, looked out over all the faces and smiled. This was my place. This was my song.

"This song's called 'Tomorrow Land,' I wrote it a while back. Hope you like it," I said into the microphone. There was a cheer from the crowd and I heard the guitar start.

"There's a place where I roam —
That's so far away from home —
Will I stay?
Will I go?
Only you will know —"

I closed my eyes and felt the music rush through me. It didn't matter what dress I was wearing, only that I was singing my song, with Jack, on a stage in London. Really, how wild was that?

The crowd went crazy when we finished the song. Jack put down his guitar and rushed up to me. He threw his arms around my waist and picked me up, swinging me around.

He whispered, "We did it, Frank, that was perfect."

I agreed. It was totally perfect.

He felt all sweaty and hot in my arms, and I could have stayed like that all night, except Asha came on stage and Jack quickly put me down and walked over to her. I saw him reach down to hug her, but she said something and stepped away from him before he could. Then Jack followed her off the stage.

Walking down the corridor from the backstage area to try to find Mum, I passed a little alcove and heard someone laugh. It was quite dark, but as I stepped closer I saw Asha and a guy. I assumed it was Jack, but as he moved, I noticed his long hair and realized it was actually Sean, the drummer from the band.

I was so surprised that I automatically looked over again, just to double-check what I'd seen. It was then that I saw the drummer lean down and kiss Asha. And she reached up, slid her arms around his neck and kissed him back.

Shocked, I rushed off.

Should I tell Jack and break his heart? Or should I keep it a secret? Surely he deserved to know what his girlfriend was up to, but would it sound like I was just trying to break them up if I told him?

I really didn't know what to do.

If you think Frankie should tell Jack she saw Asha kissing Sean, go to page 112.

If you think Frankie should keep quiet and not tell Jack she saw Asha kissing Sean, go to page 135.

Frankie GOES TO THE BEACH with her dad

Chapter Three

"Frankie, you're early!" Dad sounded surprised when he opened the front door on Thursday morning. I'd stopped using my own key after meeting Jan in the bathroom, even though Dad kept telling me it was fine.

I smiled at his overreaction. I wasn't usually that late. "I guess I'm just feeling organized. Probably won't last long."

"Well, I like it," said Dad. I put my guitar down in the hallway and he helped me with my heavy backpack. "Whoa, what have you got in here?"

"Few things." The truth was I'd packed for every kind of weather, and I'd thrown in some nice clothes just in case we did anything other than go to the beach. I didn't want Jan to think I only owned the old pair of shorts and T-shirt I usually wore all summer.

As I walked into the house, Dad hurried in front of me. "Um, there's someone I'd like you to meet."

Yet another secret girlfriend? I whirled around. "What happened to Jan?" I blurted out.

"Nothing," Dad said, laughing, as he led me into the family room. "She's upstairs getting ready."

"Oh. Then who am I meeting?" I asked, still confused.

"Me," said a voice.

I looked around the door into the family room and there, sitting on the couch, was a girl who looked about my age.

Before we could introduce ourselves, Jan hurried down the stairs and did it for us.

"Frankie, this is my daughter, Ellie," she said.

"What?" I asked, much louder than I'd intended. If Jan really had a daughter, why wouldn't Dad have told me?

"Ellie's coming with us to the beach," added Dad, watching me to check my reaction.

"Oh," I managed to say, my head spinning.

"They only just told me about you, too," said Ellie, standing up and walking over. "They seemed to think it would be a great idea to surprise us." She smiled like she found the whole thing amusing.

"Well, I'm definitely surprised," I said, trying to smile back at her.

"No kidding," she said.

"We thought this could be a chance for you to really get to know each other," explained Dad. "You can keep each other company."

Ellie and I looked at each other.

"Apparently we're sharing a room," said Ellie. "But don't worry, I don't snore."

"Frankie does," Dad piped up.

I glared at him. "Only when I have a cold!"

"Well, now that we're all here, we can head off," said Jan. She took Dad by the arm and started leading him out of the room, leaving me and Ellie alone.

Ellie was taller than me, with long, straight hair. The sort of hair I'd always wanted, particularly when mine was being completely unreasonable. She had gorgeous golden-brown skin, like she belonged on the beach. I bet she didn't burn as easily as I did, or get as many freckles. She was wearing a strappy green sundress, which I eyed enviously. If I wore something like that in the summer, my shoulders would end up looking like two cooked lobsters.

"How old are you?" Ellie asked.

"Nearly fourteen," I said.

"So I'm older," she said. "I turned fourteen in June. Any other siblings waiting to jump out and surprise me?"

"Nope. What about you?"

She shook her head. "As far as I know there's just me."

As she flicked her blonde hair over her shoulders, I saw that her ears were pierced. Lucky her. Maybe I could ask Dad again about getting mine done. It would be awesome if I could come back from vacation with pierced ears.

Then Dad called out, "Come on, girls, in the car."

Girls. Great. He made it sound like I had an insta-sister.

I was glad Jan had a big car because it meant I wasn't crammed up close next to Ellie. We both stacked some of our things in the middle of the backseat, like a little fence between us. It wasn't that I particularly minded her coming to the beach, but I wasn't going to go out of my way to be her BFF. I was annoyed with Dad for not telling me about her. It felt like what had happened with Jan all over again.

From the backseat, I watched Jan put her hand on Dad's knee while he was driving. It made me uncomfortable. She seemed okay, but I'd only met her twice: once in the bathroom and the second time at dinner. I wasn't used to the idea of Dad having a girlfriend, and now I was expected to watch her putting her hand on my dad's knee, and hang out with her daughter for the next ten days.

Maybe I would have been better off going to London with Mum. At least then I wouldn't have had to share a room with a girl I didn't know and see my dad with his new girlfriend every day.

I wondered if Ellie had spent more time with Dad and Jan than I had, and how she felt about her mum having a new boyfriend. I guess I had the whole vacation to find out.

A couple of hours later we pulled into a driveway and Jan turned around and smiled at both of us. "We're here. Ellie, can you show Frankie around?"

"Sure," said Ellie, and climbed out of the car.

The house was beautiful. It was painted white and was old-fashioned looking. I spotted a hammock hanging between two trees in the backyard. There didn't seem to be any fences, so the yards just ran together from one house to the next.

"The beach is just down at the end of the street,"

said Ellie. "Can you surf?"

"Nope. But Dad said I could learn while I was here."

"Good luck with that," said Ellie, smiling. Then she shrugged. "Maybe you're not as unco as I am. I can't even stand up on a board!"

"I always wanted to learn with my best friend, Gen," I said, wishing I could be sharing a room with Gen instead of this girl I hardly knew. I sighed, following Ellie down some stairs.

"We're sharing this room," said Ellie as we came to an enormous bedroom. Actually, it was more like a whole wing than a bedroom. Two huge beds, a sliding door that opened onto a balcony, and our own bathroom!

"Wow!" I couldn't help saying.

"Yeah, I guess. Mum bought it after she and Dad split. We don't come down here that much during the year, but we always try and use it over the summer. Usually my best friend comes with us."

Obviously she'd rather be sharing the room with her best friend too. That was fine. I knew how she felt.

"Have you got friends here?" I asked, suddenly

imagining that she'd be off with a whole bunch of people and I'd be hanging out on my own in surf school every day.

"Yeah. We meet up on the beach," she said, sitting on the bed under the window. "And there are heaps of parties."

I groaned. Dad would never let me go to a party if he didn't know the family or he hadn't already checked that there would be a parent present. He was even more full-on about that stuff than Mum was. I wondered if Jan was very strict with Ellie. It didn't sound like it.

"What's wrong?" Ellie asked.

I shrugged. "Dad has rules."

"You can always get around rules," she said.

"Not my dad's." I spoke from experience. Gen and I had tried in the past, but no amount of begging ever seemed to work. It was easier to just accept that his rules were his rules.

"Just don't tell him," said Ellie. "My dad has no idea what I get up to."

"Really?" I asked, not being able to imagine what

that was like.

"He lives in Sydney with his new girlfriend so I hardly see him. To be honest, I think he prefers me not taking up too much of his time."

"Oh," I said, feeling kind of lucky that both my parents always wanted me around.

"You wait. It'll happen to you too. Now that your dad has my mum he won't want you around as much," she said, like it was a matter of fact.

Was she right? I guess I'd never known Dad to have a girlfriend since he and Mum split up, so I suppose anything was possible. But I didn't like how confident Ellie sounded about it. She didn't even know my dad.

Then, as if she didn't want to talk about it anymore, Ellie suddenly jumped up off the bed. "Beach?"

The beach *was* just down at the end of the street. It was one of those sprawling beaches that seem to go on forever.

We chose a spot on the sand and I dropped my things and spread out my towel. I really wanted to just run straight into the water but I wasn't sure if I should wait for Ellie or not.

She was wearing a green patterned bikini that I instantly wished I owned. Mum told me I could get a bikini when I could buy one myself, but since I'd just had to spend my busking savings on a new bike, it would be ages before I'd have enough money saved.

"Are you going in?" I asked Ellie, assuming she'd say no because she'd just pulled a book out of her bag.

But she surprised me by standing up and tossing her sunglasses onto the sand. "Yeah, why not?"

As we walked down to the water, I could see a bunch of kids further along the beach. One of them yelled out to Ellie and she waved.

"Actually, I'm just going to go and say hi," she said and started walking off towards them, leaving me on my own.

I loved swimming in the sea so I didn't care that I was alone, but I thought it was weird that she didn't even ask me to go with her.

Maybe she really didn't plan on hanging out with me at all this vacation.

I guess, from her perspective, it must have been pretty hard to find out about me. It was bad enough having to share my dad, but Ellie had to share her mum, her room, her beach house and her friends.

Still, I hoped things would be okay. If this vacation got all messy, I couldn't just call Mum to come and get me. She was in London, so I was stuck here. And that meant I had to find a way to enjoy myself. I figured the sea was a pretty good place to start.

I ran straight into the water and dived under a wave. I came up, then dived straight under another. I'd always loved being in water. Even though I'd given up the swim team, I still loved swimming, so I went a bit further out to avoid all the little kids on their boogie boards. A big wave came and I duck-dived under it, trying not to get sucked up and tumbled around. When I surfaced, another wave was headed towards me.

"Hey!" someone yelled. I looked up just in time to

see a surfer flying past, right next to my head.

I dived under the wave and a cute boy about my age paddled up next to me on his surfboard. "You're too far out. I almost hit you," he said. "Swimmers should be that side of the flags."

"Sorry," I said, feeling embarrassed. I turned to see where the flags were and realized how far I'd drifted.

"Are you okay to get back in?" he said.

"Yeah, I'll be fine," I said.

"Okay, see ya around."

I watched him paddling out further. He looked really confident in the water, like he knew exactly what he was doing. I wondered if Ellie knew who he was. He disappeared over a wave and then bobbed up again on the other side. Then I saw him catch a wave all the way into shore. It looked so fun. I decided that if Ellie was going to leave me on my own, then at least I could learn how to ride a board. I'd talk to Dad later about signing me up for lessons.

Walking back along the beach, the sun was shining in my eyes so I didn't see Ellie waving until I was right up close. She was sitting with three other kids.

"Frankie!" she called out. I felt a bit shy walking over to a group I didn't know. "This is Luke and Richie, and Sarah. This is Frankie," said Ellie, introducing us.

"Hi," I said, squinting into the sun. I couldn't really see their faces, just a bunch of outlines. Then one of the boys stood up and starting shaking his towel.

"Luke!" yelled the girl. "You're getting sand in my eyes."

"So close them," he said, laughing.

As he stepped closer to me, I could see his face. He was cute, and wearing a wetsuit unzipped to his waist. His hair was curly and blond and he had amazing blue eyes. It was the surfer boy! He must have realized I was the swimmer at about the same time, because he said, "Oh, it's you."

"Do you guys know each other?" asked Ellie, sounding surprised.

"Yeah. Well, no. I almost knocked her out on my

board before," he said.

The girl called Sarah groaned and stood up. "You're a pain, Luke. You think you own the beach."

"No, I don't. Swimmers just think they can go anywhere," he said, sounding cross.

"Ice cream?" said Ellie loudly, obviously trying to change the subject. It worked. Suddenly everyone got up and started grabbing their stuff.

I wasn't sure what I was supposed to do. Nobody had actually asked me to come so I started heading back to the path, when I heard Luke call out behind me, "The surf club's this way."

I looked around and they were all waiting for me. "Oh. Okay," I said, feeling like the new kid.

It was pretty weird walking along with a group of kids I didn't know. It wasn't like Ellie and I were friends either. I felt like I'd just crashed a party. They all talked over each other, especially Luke and Sarah. I couldn't work out what their deal was. Maybe they were going out, but they seemed to argue all the time.

As we walked into the surf club, I realized with a

panic that I had no money with me. The others were all ordering ice cream, and I was going to have to pretend that I didn't want one.

"Frankie? What are you having?" asked Ellie.

"Um. I'm fine," I said softly.

"Nah, it's tradition," Luke said.

I stepped close to Ellie. "I didn't bring any cash," I said quietly.

She shrugged. "I've got money. My treat. Quick," she said, getting ready to order.

"Whatever. I don't mind," I said, pleased she wasn't making a big deal of it. It made me like her just a bit more.

She handed me a cone. "Chocolate and strawberry."

I smiled as I took it. Weird. They were the two flavors I would have ordered. "Thanks."

"No worries," she said and started to walk outside. The others were sitting on the balcony in metal chairs, looking out across the beach. Nobody was talking much, they were too busy trying to eat their ice cream before it melted.

Then Luke jumped up and yelled, "Look. Dolphins!"

He pointed out to sea and a big drip of his ice cream landed on Sarah's shoulder.

"Urgh! Luke!" she yelled loudly, causing other people to turn and stare.

"Sorry. Accident. As if I'd waste my ice cream on you!"

He tried to wipe it all off her shoulder with a towel, but just smeared it everywhere. She handed him her cone. "I'm going to go and clean myself up. Don't eat mine!"

He nodded, but as soon as she'd left, he started licking madly.

"Luke," said Ellie.

"I have to. It's melting. Did anyone see the dolphins?"

I was trying to, but all I could see were sets of waves breaking.

Luke led me across to the railing at the edge of the balcony and pointed. "There. See?"

"Nope." I said. He touched the side of my head and turned it a bit so I was looking in a different direction. "There."

And just as he said it, a dolphin jumped out of the water and into the air.

I squealed. "Yes! Oh, it's beautiful." I'd only ever seen dolphins once and it was years ago. Behind it, a whole pod of dolphins breached the waves. It was like they were performing just for us.

"Give it, Luke," said Sarah as she walked up behind us. Luke spun around and guiltily handed over what was left of her ice cream. She stared at it and then at him. "You ate it all!"

"Not all. And it was dripping. I saved it for you."

She took the almost-empty cone from him and looked at me. "Have you got any brothers or sisters?" she asked.

"Oh, you guys are …" I trailed off. So they were brother and sister. It sort of explained how they were with each other. "Nope, there's just me."

"You're so lucky!" she said. "I have three brothers. They drive me crazy. All of them. I can't stand it sometimes."

I thought about Gen and her brothers. As much as

they could annoy her, she also loved them. All that fun. Sometimes when my mum and dad were both super busy with work, I really envied her. It could get lonely being an only child with single parents.

Luke pretended to look offended. "I'm an awesome big brother! I taught you to surf."

Sarah laughed. "Oh yeah! You paddled off and left me, remember?"

Luke rolled his eyes at her. "You can't blame the teacher if you're lame."

I smiled. I liked the banter between them.

"See what I mean, Frankie?" said Sarah as she ate the last of her cone.

I sort of did. But actually Luke seemed pretty fun. We walked back to the chairs and sat down with Ellie and Richie. She was laughing and playing with her hair, and I got the feeling she liked him.

"Hey, I'm having a party tomorrow night. You guys should come," said Luke, nodding towards me and Ellie.

"Actually, *we* are having a party," said Sarah, glaring at her brother.

"Cool. We'll be there," said Ellie straightaway.

I didn't say anything, but I knew it was unlikely *I'd* be there.

Dad was lying in the hammock when we came back from the beach. I gave him a push as I went past and he opened an eye to look at me.

Making sure I was alone, he said quietly, "You and Ellie seem to be getting along."

"Yeah. She's nice," I said, watching her go into the house. "But why didn't you tell me about her?"

"I'm sorry," he said. "I thought it was for the best. I didn't want you to feel strange about coming on vacation with us."

I was never very good at staying cross with Dad, but this time I think I was allowed to. "You don't like it when I don't tell you the truth. It's a bit rough, Dad."

"It's not like I lied, Frankie. It's more an omission of fact," he said with a smile.

"You should have told me the truth," I said, hurt

that he wasn't taking it seriously.

"Sorry. It's all new, Frankie. There are no rules about how to do this," he said. And then he asked, like it was really important to him that I said yes, "Do you like Jan?"

"I don't really know her yet," I said, and then regretted it because he looked really disappointed. "Dad. It's just early, that's all."

"I know. But I want you guys …" he said and then stopped. "You're right, it's early. But it'll be good for all of us to get to know each other some more. And for you and me to spend some quality time together, won't it?"

I wondered how it was going to work. Would Jan and Ellie like doing the things Dad and I did together, like singing and playing guitar, or watching bad horror movies and listening to old vinyl? Or would Jan and Ellie do their own thing?

Then Jan called out from the house, "Lunch is ready!"

Dad and I looked at each other. I was starving. And

obviously, so was he, because he was in such a hurry to get out of the hammock he sort of threw himself onto the ground.

"Ow," he said as I helped him up. Then he half pushed me out of the way and yelled, "Race you."

Jan looked a bit surprised as we chased each other in through the front door, letting it bang behind us. I made it to the table first, sliding my way into the seat.

The table was full of food. There were salads, sandwiches, platters of fruit and cheese. I was impressed. Neither of my parents was a good cook so I was sort of used to getting my own lunch and sometimes even my dinner, which was usually just pasta and cheese.

"Yum! Thanks, Jan. This looks amazing," I said.

Jan laughed. "It wasn't me!"

Surprised, I looked at Dad. He nodded. "She's a worse cook than I am," he said and earned himself a light whack on the arm.

"At least I don't burn toast!" said Jan, smiling. "Ellie did it, Frankie. She's a great cook."

I looked at Ellie to check her reaction. "What can I

say? I'm awesome," she said, smiling.

Dad was piling his plate so high I couldn't imagine how he was going to get through it all.

"This is delicious," I said a few moments later, through a mouthful of salad.

"So, Frankie and I have been invited to a party tomorrow night," Ellie dropped, while everyone was focused on eating.

Dad looked up sharply. "I don't think so, Ellie."

I rolled my eyes at Ellie as if to say, *I told you.*

"Why?" she asked Dad, ignoring me.

"Not unless there's a parent present and I know the family," said Dad. "That's just house rules."

"Well, not this house," argued Ellie. I was impressed. She wasn't being rude, just honest.

Dad looked across at Jan to get her opinion.

"Where's the party, El?" asked Jan.

"At Sarah and Luke Mackinnon's," she answered.

Jan turned back to Dad. "It's at the end of the street. I know the family and they've been coming down here longer than us. They're lovely kids."

Dad must have felt like he was losing because he frowned. "But *I* don't know them," he said softly.

As much as I wanted him to say yes, I sort of felt sorry for him. It was like he was being outsmarted and he was running out of arguments.

"Please, Dad. We'll take our phones," I said, actually using my pleading voice.

He was obviously thinking hard about it, but then he shook his head. "Sorry, girls. I'm sure there will be other parties. Just not tomorrow."

Even though I always knew he'd say no, I was really disappointed. But Ellie's jaw dropped, like she was stunned that something like this could happen.

"Mum?" said Ellie, obviously thinking she could get Jan to override Dad's decision. "You always let me go to parties at Luke's."

"I know, honey, but if John doesn't want Frankie to go, I can't very well let you go. Why don't we all have a movie night together?"

"But Mum! That's so unfair!" cried Ellie. "You just said you know the family, and that they're lovely kids." She turned to Dad. "Why don't you trust Mum's judgment?"

"Ellie, that's enough!" said Jan.

"Are you going to let your boyfriend make all the decisions for us from now on? He's not my father! I don't have to put up with this!" She stormed out of the kitchen and raced downstairs, slamming our bedroom door dramatically.

None of us said anything for a minute because I don't think anyone knew what to say. I just sat, staring down at my plate.

"I'll go talk to her," said Jan finally, getting up from the table.

When she had left the room, Dad started clearing the plates away. "None of this is easy, is it, Frankie?" he said, and sighed.

"So, let's just sneak out," said Ellie later that afternoon, flicking her long blonde hair over her shoulders.

I was sitting on my bed strumming my guitar. "Nah," I said, not looking up.

"Come on. They won't know. Trust me, they won't have any idea that we're not just asleep."

I looked up at Ellie, with her tanned skin and long hair. She acted like she was much older than me. I'd never sneaked out. I sort of just accepted that my parents had strict rules about parties and pierced ears because they let me do most of the things I wanted to do, like playing guitar or hanging out with Gen.

"It'll be fine. Mum lets me go to parties like this all the time. She won't care. It's only your dad who is being a freak about it. Besides, don't you want to see Luke?" asked Ellie, raising an eyebrow.

I shrugged. How did she know I thought he was cute? I wasn't going to talk about boys with her yet. I'd only just met her. Maybe we'd become good friends, but it was too early to tell.

"I'm going to walk into town," I said to Ellie, changing the subject. I put down my guitar.

"Well, I'm going to have a nap," she said, stretching

out on her bed.

I was pleased she wasn't coming. I felt like some time away from everyone.

I grabbed my purse, phone, hat, sunglasses, sunscreen and water. I didn't want any more freckles this summer so I had to try to make sure I didn't get too much sun. I left Dad a note and walked down onto the beach.

Where the walking path came out on the beach, I kicked off my flip-flops and stuck them in the sand so I didn't have to carry them with me. It was something Dad and I always did on our walks along the beach each summer.

I didn't know how long it would take to walk into town. Ellie had told me I could just walk along the beach, past the surf club and I'd get to town, so I figured it couldn't be that far.

I reached the surf club and instead of walking up the hill, I kept going along the sand. There were heaps of rocks and I had to climb over them, dodging the sharp bits with my bare feet. As I jumped back down onto the sand, I saw a man and a woman walking towards me, holding hands. I knew it was Dad and Jan, because he was wearing his funny old straw beach hat that he'd been wearing since I was a kid.

There was something about watching them walking together that made me realize they were a real couple. I had no memories of Mum and Dad ever being like that.

"Where's Ellie?" asked Jan as they got closer.

"Sleeping," I said.

"She should have come with you," said Jan.

Or she should have gone walking with you because she's your daughter, I wanted to say. But I didn't.

"Want some company, kiddo?" asked Dad.

Touched that he'd offered, even though he was out walking with Jan, I shook my head. "I'm fine."

"Righto. We'll see you back at the house for dinner." Dad gave me a kiss and I wandered off towards town. I knew Ellie was wrong about Dad. He didn't want to get rid of me. There was room for all of us in his life.

Town was actually just eight shops, and a pub. No one seemed to look at me strangely for walking around in bare feet. I guess it was a pretty relaxed little place.

It took me about five minutes to look around. I bought some electric blue nail polish and a postcard for Mum. Even though she was away, I wanted to let her know I was missing her.

I walked back along the beach and sat down on the warm sand to watch the surfers. The sun was starting to go down and it was beautiful.

A surfer came out of the water and walked up the beach towards me, carrying his board. As he got closer, I realized it was Luke.

"Hey," he said, as he dropped down on the sand next to me. He flicked his hair and sandy water hit me in the face.

"Argh, thanks!"

"Sorry," he said, grinning at me. He had such a cute smile. "Can you surf?" he asked.

"I wish. I want to learn."

"I can teach you," he said and I laughed. "What?" he said, sounding offended.

"Nothing, it's just after Sarah said –"

"Yeah, well, she has no balance. She doesn't listen to the waves."

"Right," I said, wondering how you listen to waves.

"It's easy. You'd be fine," he said.

I heard my phone beep and I rifled around in my bag. It was a text from Gen.

I cannot believe your dad kept Jan's daughter a secret! We must discuss!

As much as I wanted to talk to her, I didn't want to do it in front of Luke so I dropped my phone back into my bag.

"You coming to our party?" he asked.

I shook my head. "Nope."

"You have to!" he said, obviously surprised anyone would miss one of his parties.

"Dad said no," I said, not bothering to make up an excuse. I figured that Ellie would tell him the truth anyway.

"Is Ellie coming?" he asked.

"I'm not sure. She wants us to sneak out."

"Are you going to?" he asked.

Before I could answer, my phone rang.

"Popular," said Luke.

"Hey," I said. It was Dad.

"We're waiting for you, Frankie. Jan's cooked dinner," said Dad.

"Sorry, be there in a minute." I grabbed my bag. "Gotta go, Luke. Have a great party."

He started following me but I was in a hurry.

"Make sure you come tomorrow night!" yelled Luke after me.

I smiled to myself as I wandered up the path. How often did cute surfer boys invite me to parties? It would be so cool to go. But I just didn't know if I could risk sneaking out.

Dinner was a bit weird. Maybe we'd all had too much sun, or maybe it was because of the argument at lunchtime, but nobody said much. We sort of ate dinner and then went off to do our own thing. I'd been hoping we could play some rowdy family board games because that's what Dad and I usually liked doing on vacation, but Ellie slunk off to bed with her laptop and headphones, and Jan dragged Dad away to sit on the balcony.

I was going to play my guitar but I didn't want to annoy Ellie, so instead I messaged Gen.

Sharing a room with Ellie Who Hates Me. But on plus side, have met cute surfer boy, and been invited to his party. No way I'm allowed to go but Ellie wants us to sneak out.

Gen wrote back:

OMG! Sounds amazing. Most exciting thing that has happened here is that one of my cousins was stung by a jellyfish and we had to get vinegar from a fish-and-chips shop to pour on it. PS Am sure Ellie doesn't hate you!

I missed Gen. It was going to be a long vacation without her around.

I woke up stupidly early because there were birds

singing right outside the bedroom window. I tried to go back to sleep but I couldn't, so I grabbed my bathing suit and towel and went down to the beach for an early morning swim.

The water was icy getting in, but I made myself dive through the waves. Out past the breakers, with early morning sunlight glinting off the water, I felt so alive and happy that none of yesterday's weirdness with Jan and Ellie even seemed to matter.

By the time I came back to the house I was starving. I made some toast, which I managed not to burn, and perched up at the counter to eat it. The house was quiet and I had no idea where everybody was.

Ellie wandered out in her tank top and shorts as I was unloading the dishwasher.

"Morning," she said sleepily.

"The beach was gorgeous this morning," I said. I knew my hair was all salty and crunchy. Frizzy hair didn't like salt water. It made it go even more matted and thick.

"Too early for swimming," she said, even though it was nearly eleven.

"Have you seen Dad?" I asked. Just as I did, he and Jan wandered in, wearing very similar pajamas.

Dad gave me a bit of a hug.

"Where's my red tea cup?" asked Jan, looking in the now-emptied dishwasher.

"Oh, I put it in that cupboard," I said, pointing to the one behind her.

She smiled. "Thanks, Frankie, but the cups go in that one over there," she said, pointing to another cupboard.

"I was just trying to help," I said, sounding crankier than I'd meant to.

Dad looked at me strangely. "Jan wasn't telling you off, honey. She was just explaining which cupboard the cups go in."

I nodded. I knew that, but when I unloaded the dishwasher at Mum's house, she never minded if I put things in the wrong cupboards. She was just happy that I'd helped.

Maybe I was just really missing Mum.

Jan had made arrangements for her and Dad to go to a winery for lunch so Ellie and I found ourselves alone in the house.

I was planning on heading back to the beach, but Ellie suggested we sit outside on the balcony and do our nails. I painted hers pink and she did mine electric blue.

"Awesome color, Frankie," said Ellie, looking at my toes.

"They look like little jelly beans," I said, wriggling them.

Ellie wriggled her pink ones. "I want blue now," she said, and stuck her feet up onto the chair so I could repaint them.

"Have you got a boyfriend?" asked Ellie, as I finished one foot and she looked at it.

"Nope. You?" I asked, starting on her other foot.

She shook her head.

"But you do have cool blue toes," I said, as we both looked at her finished nails.

"Yeah. I like them. Thanks," she said, smiling at me. "Swim?"

"My favorite word!" I said, jumping up to go and grab my stuff.

But there was no need to hurry, because nothing was quick with Ellie. She moved as slowly as a sloth. First, she packed her bag, and then changed her mind about the bathing suit she was going to wear. Then she wanted to take some lunch with us, so she repacked her bag, but couldn't find the book she wanted to read. But for some reason it didn't irritate me at all. Maybe that meant I liked her company?

Dad and Jan didn't get back until nearly dinnertime, and even though Dad apologized for having been gone all day, I didn't really get the sense that the rest of the vacation was going to be any different. I started wondering how much he had actually wanted me there, and how much I'd just been asked because Ellie was coming and Dad and Jan wanted someone to hang out with her so they could go off and do their thing.

"Red or blue?" asked Ellie, holding up two dresses.

"Blue," I said, staring enviously at all the clothes she'd unpacked. I thought I'd brought heaps of stuff with me, but my stuff was boring compared to hers.

"You can wear the red one if you like. It'd look great on you," said Ellie, tossing the other dress across to my bed.

"I can't go," I said, throwing the dress back.

"Yes, you can," she answered as she threw it back again.

I shook my head. "I can't," I said, picking up the dress to throw it back. It was gorgeous. Soft, summery and light, and not like anything I had. I was a jeans girl. Or shorts. T-shirts. Comfortable easy clothes. This was much more glamorous than anything I'd usually put on, and I wished I could wear it.

"Whatevs," said Ellie as she walked past and shut the bathroom door. I'm sure she thought I was acting like a little kid, just doing whatever Dad told me. And to be honest, the idea of hanging out alone while Ellie went to a party with Luke did make me feel like a loser.

I unlocked the door that led out to the balcony. It was one of those hot summer nights where it felt even warmer than it had during the day. I could hear my dad laughing and glasses clinking, and I realized that he and Jan were drinking wine on the balcony just above us.

"How are the girls getting along, do you think?" I heard Jan ask.

"Really well," said Dad, and I wondered what he was basing that on, given he'd hardly spent any time with us. I heard Jan agree with him and then add, "I'm glad Frankie came. She can keep Ellie company. It gives us more time together."

I was almost holding my breath, waiting for Dad to disagree, but he didn't. Instead he said, "Yeah, it's perfect. We should go to that little restaurant on the beach tomorrow. The girls will be okay."

Hurt, I backed quietly inside and shut the door behind me. So I was right. I *had* just been brought along as a friend for Ellie. So much for Dad saying he'd been looking forward to spending time with me this vacation.

As Ellie came out of the shower, I rifled around in my bag for my book. I didn't particularly want to talk to anyone.

"Can you zip me up?" asked Ellie with her back to me. I reached over and zipped up her dress. She looked amazing. Her hair was hanging straight down and her dress was just slightly fitted. She was wearing flip-flops and she looked all brown and sun-kissed. I couldn't see a single freckle.

"You could come for an hour," she said. "Tell your dad you're going to bed because you've got a headache and then just sneak out through the balcony door."

I didn't want to have this conversation again, so I said nothing.

"Seriously, they won't even notice we're gone. They're going to watch some boring movie and then they'll go to bed," said Ellie lightly.

She was probably right. Dad and Jan did just seem to want to be alone. It wasn't like we'd be hanging out playing board games together.

Ellie must have sensed I was wavering, because she pounced. "Just an hour. I promise. Please, Frankie. I hate going to parties on my own. And I told Luke you were coming."

She made it sound so simple. Dad wouldn't know if I sneaked out for an hour. It was *just* down the street. And it would be heaps of fun. And Luke was really cute. Plus, if Dad had brought me along to keep Ellie company then shouldn't I just do that?

But if I did go to the party, I'd be deliberately ignoring Dad's rules, sneaking out and lying to him. I would be in so much trouble if he ever found out.

Should I go? Or not?

If you think Frankie should go to the party, go to page 155.

If you think Frankie should stay at home, go to page 173.

Frankie TELLS JACK about Asha

Chapter Four

"Where have you been? Have you seen Asha?" asked Jack, walking towards me.

This was my chance. I just had to blurt out what I'd seen, tell him so he knew what his girlfriend was *really* like. But he looked so pleased about the gig that I didn't want to bring him down. Besides, what if I had gotten it wrong somehow? Then I'd just look like I was trying to break them up.

"Think she's somewhere backstage. Great gig," I said, knowing that would distract him.

His eyes shone as he smiled back. "Yeah, it was brilliant. When you guys were backstage just now, the manager offered us a residency."

"That's awesome!" I said, totally understanding what it meant to him. I'd be pumped too if a band I played with was offered a regular gig.

"What's awesome?" said a voice behind me. I knew it was Asha without even having to turn around.

"We got a residency!" said Jack, grinning at his girlfriend.

"Hope they're paying us a bit better than they did tonight," she said, causing Jack to look crushed. I couldn't believe she didn't understand what it meant to him. If she did understand, then why would she be so cruel?

"Pity you won't be around to sing, Frankie," she said coolly. Then she added, "Nice dress."

Jack looked from one of us to the other. "You two could be twins."

"Hardly. I'm not wearing sneakers!" said Asha.

I stuck my foot out. "They're Converse. My faves."

And they were. Bright purple. Comfy, cool. And Gen had some exactly the same. I didn't care what Asha thought about my shoes. I liked them.

I waited for the next sarcastic comment, but instead she surprised me by nodding. "Yeah, my feet are killing me. Wish I'd worn sneakers."

"Oh," I said, because I had nothing else to say. What do you say to the girl who's dating the boy you like when you know she's cheating on him?

Feeling totally uncomfortable, I started looking around for Mum but the shop was almost empty and I couldn't see her or Tina anywhere.

"We're going to our mate Sammy's place for a bit of a party," Jack said to me. "If you want to come. His dad still plays in bands and he's pretty relaxed – he doesn't mind a bunch of kids turning up and playing loud music."

"Nah, I'm going home," I said, not wanting to be around either of them.

"No, you're not. I already cleared it with The Mums," said Jack, picking up his guitar and stand. "They said it was cool, as long as we're home by ten thirty."

"Maybe she wants to go home, Jack," said Asha, clearly wanting me to.

"Don't care. She played a song so she has to come. The whole band is coming," he argued.

"The whole band?" asked Asha, and I wondered if she was asking about Sean.

The thought of seeing her have to deal with Jack and Sean at the same party was enough to change my mind. I grabbed Jack's guitar stand from him. "Actually, maybe I will come for a bit."

It wasn't far to walk to Sammy's, but it was freezing. And it just confirmed the fact that I could never live in London permanently.

At home I didn't need to wear a hundred layers just to walk to a party at night.

Asha had done her disappearing trick again so I was walking with Jack, who hadn't stopped talking about how amazing the gig was. I agreed with everything he'd said, but I wished he'd stop thinking about music for two seconds and concentrate on his girlfriend a bit more. Maybe then I wouldn't need to tell him that she was cheating on him. Maybe he'd just know.

As we walked up the steps to Sammy's dad's house, music was already pumping loud enough to be heard on the street. I felt weird going to a party with Jack and Asha, but at least it sounded like it was going to be an awesome party. I might even get to dance.

Inside there were kids everywhere. It was like the whole gig had just turned up. Jack seemed to know everyone, but he was pretty good about introducing me, so I felt totally comfortable. When a song came on that I loved, I grabbed his hand and told him he had to come and dance with me. Laughing, he shook his head and tried to escape. "I'm an awful dancer, Frankie."

"I don't care. I can't dance on my own," I said, pulling him further along the hall.

Jack was right about the dancing. Awful with a capital A. But for some reason it just made me like him that little bit more. I was so used to seeing him being good at things that it was nice seeing him try something he wasn't great at.

A song came on that Gen and I had worked out dance moves to, and I was trying to teach them to Jack when he stopped dancing altogether.

"Come on, it's not that hard," I said, thinking he was finding it too difficult to move one leg to the right and then the other.

But he shook his head. "Sorry, it's not that," he said, looking past me. "Is that Asha and Sean?"

I turned around to see Asha dancing with Sean. They were laughing at each other and obviously having a great time.

"Yeah," I said.

"Let's go over," said Jack, not waiting to hear what I thought of that idea.

He started pushing his way through all the people dancing, but I grabbed his arm and pulled him back.

"No, wait a minute," I said, knowing it was now or never.

"What?" he asked.

"Um, I want to tell you something. Can we go somewhere a bit quieter?"

He frowned at me, "Can't it wait, Frank?"

I shook my head. *Nope. Not anymore.*

He finally followed me out of the room and down the hall to the kitchen. I could still hear the music but it wasn't as loud or crazy as it had been in the living room. Jack leaned against the fridge and looked at me, waiting.

"I saw something tonight at the gig. Asha ... and ... um ..." I trailed off. I *so* didn't want to be the person telling him this, but what choice did I have? Even though I couldn't understand what he saw in her, I still didn't want him to have to watch her flirt with someone else and not know what was really going on.

"Yeah?" said Jack, getting impatient.

I took a deep breath. "She was kissing Sean. Backstage. I saw them after the gig."

Jack made a funny face and then half laughed. "Don't be silly, Frankie. Asha wouldn't do that. And Sean's one of my mates."

I shrugged, surprised at his reaction. I just assumed he'd believe me, but I guess hearing your girlfriend had been kissing one of your best friends wasn't something to be expected. "I know what I saw, Jack."

"I understand it's been hard for you finding out about Asha –"

"Oh no. I'm not making this up," I said, angry. *As if* I'd invent this just to get back at him. "Forget it, Jack." I stormed off, wishing I'd just let him get hurt.

As I ran down the hallway, I bashed into a tall guy. "Sorr–"

"Whoa! You're the singer, aren't you?"

"Yeah," I said, wondering who he was.

"Great song," he said, smiling. "I'm Sammy. I live here."

I smiled back at him. He was super cute. He had really bright blue eyes and short, neat hair, and where Jack was scruffy like most of the boys back home, this guy was wearing a shirt with buttons and nice pants. He was dressed more like my dad. But still, he was gorgeous.

"Hey. Great party, Sammy. But I've gotta go," I said, suddenly wishing I could stay and talk to him. It would be nice to chat to someone who wasn't Jack.

"Where are you going?" he asked. "Another party?"

I laughed at that. "No. I'm staying at Jack's. I'm just going home."

"Frankie!" I heard Jack call after me.

"I'd better go. See ya." I hurried towards the front door.

Suddenly, I just wanted to be home. Not Jack's home. But my real home in Australia. With Gen and Dad and Mum. And then I could forget I ever came to London or saw Jack again, or got messed up in his stupid relationship.

As I opened the front door to head outside, I realized I wasn't really sure where I was, or how to get home. I walked out onto the street, still annoyed with Jack but half expecting him to come after me. Surely he wouldn't let me walk home alone. But he didn't appear.

I turned down the way we had come, and was almost at the end of the block when I heard footsteps behind me. I spun around in the freezing night air, and saw it was Sammy running after me.

"Hi," he said, puffing slightly. His breath formed clouds of condensation in the air. "I told Jack I'd walk you home. He wasn't sure you knew the way."

"Right. I don't, really. But aren't you leaving your own party?" I asked, feeling a bit pleased that Sammy was walking me home, partly because all the streets looked the same and I had no idea which one to turn down, and partly because he was *very* cute and a good distraction from Jack.

"Nobody will even notice," he said. "Besides, I want to know if you have more songs like 'Tomorrow Land.'"

"Oh. Yeah, heaps," I said, pleased he'd remembered the name of it.

"Then maybe you'll sing them to me before you fly home," he said with another smile.

"Are you a muso too?" I asked.

"Violin. Classical," he told me.

"Wow. Isn't violin impossible to play?" I said, seriously impressed. I'd actually tried to learn the violin at school but I was never very good at it. Guitar came much more naturally to me. But I loved the sound of violin.

We walked through the quiet streets and Sammy told me all about how he and Jack had met in a music class when they were really little and then ended up at school together and stayed friends.

"Are you still at school together?" I said.

"No. I started at a classical music school last year. I get to practice violin all day."

"Really? No math?" It sounded too good to be true. Writing and playing music all day was my dream.

"Yeah, it's great. We still have to do some work in other subjects, but mostly we compose and play."

"Wow. I'm officially jealous," I said with a smile.

"Well, this is you, Frankie Jones," said Sammy as we walked up to Jack's house.

I was a bit disappointed that we were back so quickly. I'd really enjoyed talking to him.

"So, can I drop by one day? Listen to those songs?"

I nodded. "Sure. Bring your violin."

He watched me as I walked up the stairs and fiddled around, trying to unlock the front door. It was sweet. And a bit old-fashioned. I'm pretty sure Mum would approve.

I quietly got into bed, trying not to wake Mum. As

I lay there, I decided that if Jack wanted to date Asha even though she was cheating on him, then that was his choice. I wanted nothing more to do with it.

The next day, Mum wanted me to go shopping with her to buy something she could wear to her fancy International Architecture and Design Awards. We jumped on the tube and got off at Marble Arch. When we popped up onto the street, we headed along Oxford Street, jostling with other shoppers as London whirled around us: black cabs, red buses, roasted chestnuts, beautiful buildings – and people, so many people everywhere. We went into Selfridges and Mum flew into action. Normally, she preferred pottering in home goods shops and buying little things for the kitchen and the family room. But here in London, she seemed quite happy trying on designer clothing. She found a gorgeous black dress that was perfect for the awards night.

After we'd shopped for her, we went shopping for me. I led her up Oxford Street to Topshop, which Gen and I had discovered in our shopping research. I wasn't expecting Mum to let me go crazy, but she did. I bought up big and I also found a few of the things that Gen had wanted me to get for her: a top she'd wanted and her favorite-color nail polish.

Afterwards, we found a cafe in a cool little street nearby and ordered the biggest bowls of soup they had.

Mum asked me about the gig and the party and I told her as little as I could – I didn't want to ruin our nice shopping day by getting her worried. I left out Asha kissing Sean, fighting with Jack, and Sammy walking me home. So it didn't leave much.

"Funny, I thought I heard Jack come home after you," said Mum as she finished off her soup.

"Yeah, he did. But he walked me home and went back," I said, concentrating on mopping up the last bits of pumpkin soup with my bread. I wasn't really lying. Just stretching the truth a bit, and I didn't think Jack would tell her anything different.

"You having a good time with Jack?" asked Mum.

I nodded. "Yep."

"Glad you came?" she asked in that way that she has of knowing something isn't quite right.

I smiled at her. "Yeah, course, Mum."

And it was true. I *was* glad I came. I just wasn't very happy that Jack didn't believe me about Asha, or that he was dating someone who'd cheat on him in the first place. But I was still happy to be in London, shopping and seeing new things. Plus I'd gotten to sing my own song on stage last night, so that was a bit of a highlight.

Carrying all our bags of shopping, we caught the tube from Oxford Circus back to the station near Jack's house. Mum and I laughed as we squeezed onto the tube with our bags. I loved looking around at all the different people, hearing all the different languages they were speaking, and wondering what had brought all these people to London. It was great having this adventure with my mum. Just being away from home made things feel different between us – today I'd had as much fun shopping with Mum as I usually would with Gen.

By the time we made it back to the house, we were both cold and our legs were aching. Mum went upstairs for a bath and I wasn't sure what to do. I didn't know if Jack was home or if he'd even be talking to me and I really hoped that Asha wasn't coming over. I went to make a hot chocolate to try to warm up.

"Finally! I've been waiting for you to come home," said Jack, bowling into the kitchen.

I didn't want to look at him so I concentrated on making my hot chocolate.

"You were right about Asha. She told me last night," he said, really casually, like he was telling me about the bacon sandwich he'd just eaten.

"Oh," I said, shocked. "Are you okay?"

"No. Yeah. I dunno. I'm angry with her and Sean. Hurt, actually," he said.

"Did she say why she'd cheated on you?" I asked him, thinking that if someone cheated on me I'd want to know if there was a reason.

"I didn't ask. I just broke up with her," he said.

"I'm sorry, Jack," I said, feeling like it was my fault that they'd broken up. Maybe if I hadn't told him then they would have stayed together.

Out of the corner of my eye I saw him shake his head. "I'm not. I don't know what I was thinking, Frank. She's been really mean to me and to you. I should've seen it."

I stopped stirring my hot chocolate and looked at him. He was watching me with his big eyes and floppy hair and cute, lopsided smile. I knew that look. And I realized things could be different between us now that Asha was out of the picture.

But I couldn't help remembering his reaction at the party last night when I'd told him about Asha kissing Sean. He'd thought I was making up the story just because I was jealous of her. And then, instead of apologizing, he'd left me to walk home with Sammy – who was nice, but someone I didn't even know.

I'd thought hearing that Jack and Asha had broken up would make me happy. But the way he was just telling me about it so calmly in his kitchen made it seem like it was no big deal to him at all. And it made me wonder if this was how he'd been when he'd stopped e-mailing me. Like he'd just forgotten about me. And as if our kiss, which had meant so much to me, had meant nothing to him.

"Well, I'm glad it's worked out for you, Jack," I said coolly. "I'm off to text Gen."

"I thought you'd be pleased," he said, sounding confused.

"Why?" I asked him, taking a sip of my hot chocolate; even though I knew it was hot, it almost burned my mouth.

"So we can hang out now," he said, trying a smile. "It'll be awesome. And you can play the gig on Saturday. You haven't got long to learn all the songs."

"Isn't Asha singing?" I asked.

He shook his head. "No."

Great. I was just a replacement for Asha. And I was supposed to be *happy* that he was letting me step into her shoes?

"I'm not Asha. And I don't want to sing your songs. Don't you care about anyone's feelings?"

And then, because I had nothing else to say to him, I took my hot chocolate and walked upstairs.

I was reading my book in bed, avoiding Jack and feeling warm for the first time all day, when there was a light knocking on my door. I assumed it was Jack, but as I opened it, I was really surprised to see Asha.

"Do you mind?" she asked, as she started to come in.

I wanted to say, *Yes, actually, I do mind. I don't want you in my room.* But she obviously wasn't going to give me much of a choice, and I was more than a little intrigued to know what she was doing here.

She sat down on the edge of my bed so I perched across on Mum's, not wanting to sit close to her. We looked at each other without saying anything for a minute, and it was so uncomfortable that I had to look away.

"So, I'm sure that Jack told you we broke up," she said.

I wondered if she blamed me for telling him, or maybe she didn't even know. Maybe Jack had kept that part quiet.

"Well, it was pretty dumb. Kissing Sean," she said, looking down at her nails. "It only happened that night."

"Right," I said. Now that I knew she wanted to talk about her and Jack, I wished she'd leave or that Mum would come back or that an alien would land so I didn't have to have this conversation.

"Don't you want to know why I kissed Sean?" she asked.

Did I? I didn't know.

But Asha didn't seem to care because she went on to say, "I did it because Jack had been banging on about how great you were for ages and I was sick of it. I was jealous."

That surprised me. *She* was his girlfriend! Surely *I* was the one who should have been jealous. Not her.

Then she said, "When we started going out, I knew he still liked you. But you were on the other side of the world, and you were only e-mailing each other. So I made him cut off contact with you."

Asha had made him stop? Jack had broken my heart, but he only did it because of Asha.

"And then you turned up here! You turned up in the same dress as me and sang *your* song and Jack clearly still thinks you're amazing. I just wanted to get back at him and make *him* jealous."

"We're just friends, Asha. That's all," I said.

"Yeah, maybe. But he really likes you and he thinks you're amazing and I know you've snogged before," she said. "That's why I was so mean to you."

She looked straight at me this time. "I'm sorry. It wasn't your fault that Jack talked about you so much."

I actually hadn't thought at all about how she'd felt having me here. I guess it was hard having another girl staying at her boyfriend's house.

"So just explain it all to him," I said. "He'll listen to you."

She laughed then. "No, he won't. But he'll listen to you."

"Oh," I said, as I leaned back on the bed, finally realizing why she was here. She wanted *me* to talk to him for her.

"Please, Frankie. Just explain why I did it. Tell him I was jealous. Make him understand. I really like Jack. I don't want to be with anyone else," she said, almost pleading.

I didn't know what to do. I had liked Jack for such a long time, and he'd broken my heart when he stopped e-mailing me.

But if Asha was the one who'd made him do that, maybe he did actually like me. And now that he was finally single, why would I want him to work things out with her?

She'd been horrible to me the whole time I was in London.

But I guess if I was really honest, I did feel a little bit sorry for Asha. Kissing Sean was dumb, but I could understand that she'd just been trying to make Jack jealous. And really, it was my fault he found out about her cheating on him.

But that didn't mean I had to go and sort out their breakup. Did it? And could I really do anything to fix things between them anyway?

I wasn't sure. Should I talk to Jack or not?

If you think Frankie should refuse to tell Jack about Asha's feelings, go to page 192.

If you think Frankie should tell Jack that Asha still likes him, go to page 202.

Frankie DOESN'T TELL
JACK about Asha

Chapter Four

"Where have you been? Have you seen Asha?" asked Jack, walking towards me.

It would be so easy to tell him what I'd just seen. And if I did, maybe he'd realize that he should be with me, not her. I'd never cheat on him.

But what if I was wrong? What if somehow what I thought I'd seen wasn't *actually* what I thought I'd seen? Plus, he was so happy after that awesome gig, I didn't want to be the one to ruin that.

"Think she's somewhere backstage. Great gig," I said, knowing that would distract him.

His eyes shone as he smiled back. "Yeah, it was

brilliant. When you guys were backstage just now, the manager offered us a residency."

I was so happy for him. I totally understood what music meant to Jack, and the fact that I could be a tiny part of tonight was pretty exciting.

"We're going to our mate Sammy's place for a bit of a party," Jack said to me. "His dad still plays in bands and he's pretty relaxed – he doesn't mind a bunch of kids turning up and playing loud music."

Was Jack asking me to come?

"I already cleared it with The Mums," said Jack picking up his guitar and stand. "They said it was cool, as long as we're home by ten thirty."

"Oh," I said, surprised that he cared so much about me coming that he organized it with Mum. Perhaps he was just being friendly. Or maybe he felt like he had to take me with him because I'd sung with his band. Or maybe …

Stop it, Frankie Jones! You're friends. Just friends, I reminded myself. *Jack has a girlfriend. Granted, she's not very nice. But for some reason he likes her, so I have to respect that. Don't I? Even if I'd just seen her cheat on him?*

"So, who's Sammy?" I asked.

"A good friend. We've known each other since we were four. His dad has been pretty supportive of our band. Gives us advice and stuff."

"Are we walking?" I asked, dreading how cold it was going to be now.

Handing me his guitar stand to carry, Jack shrugged. "Yeah, Sammy's place is near ours. Why?"

"Why? 'Cos it's freezing! You know in my natural environment, it's summer right now. I could have gone to the beach with Dad instead of coming here with Mum on vacation!"

"I'm glad you didn't," said Jack, looking at me with those brown eyes.

I looked away. What was it with Jack tonight? Was he flirting? This wasn't how friends usually talked to each other. Was it?

As we started heading for the door, I realized he wasn't waiting for Asha and I felt a flash of annoyance. *He* was the one who'd made it clear he was taken and expected me to forget everything that had happened in Melbourne, but now he was just leaving without her.

"Aren't you waiting for Asha?" I asked, sounding as cross as I felt.

"Oh, nah, she'll turn up," he said casually, like she was a pair of shoes. It was bad enough he'd chosen her as a girlfriend, but now he didn't even seem to care if he couldn't find her. I didn't understand him at all.

"Turn up?" I asked, tired of Jack's games.

"We've been fighting a bit," he said, shuffling his feet like he really didn't want to talk about it.

"Oh," I said. "You okay?"

Jack slung his guitar strap across his shoulder and shrugged. "Yep. All good."

It was the perfect time to tell him I'd seen Asha kissing Sean. So why didn't I? Maybe it was because the way Jack was acting made me feel that whatever was going on between them somehow involved me.

Instead of saying anything, I pushed open the front door to the record shop, and a freezing blast of wind hit me in the face. I zipped up my ridiculously large puffer jacket and started walking fast down the street.

"Where are you going?" Jack called behind me.

I was walking the wrong way. I trundled back towards Jack. "It all looks the same," I said, still a bit crabby.

"No, it doesn't," argued Jack. "Fancy bars and stuff that way. Shops and chippies this way."

"Chippies?" I asked.

Jack smiled when he realized I didn't know what he was talking about. "Come on," he said, crossing the road.

Carrying the guitar stand, I chased after him, dodging a black cab and getting tooted. It was late-ish, but there were still lots of people around. I'd always known that London was busier than the suburbs of Melbourne, but it still surprised me just how busy it really was.

Jack stopped outside a shop. "Vinegar or gravy?" he asked, handing me his guitar.

"Oh, right. Chippie," I said, finally getting that it meant a fish-and-chips shop. "Um, ketchup?" I added.

He screwed up his face. "Ew, gross," he said, disappearing inside the fish-and-chips shop.

While I waited in the arctic cold, I took a selfie and sent it to Gen. In it, I made a sad face and told her I was missing her (and the sun). After I sent it, I realized just how much. Gen was my bestie, and this was probably the longest we'd ever gone without talking. The more confused I felt about Jack, the more I wished she were here.

Jack came out and handed me a paper bag. "Sorry, no ketchup."

He tore a hole in the end of the bag and all the steam poured out. I realized I'd hardly eaten since we'd left Melbourne. I was so hungry I couldn't wait until the chips cooled down and I burned my tongue about twenty times. But they were salty and covered in vinegar and, I had to admit, delicious.

We walked along, turning here and there along rows of identical-looking houses. After a while, we turned down a tree-lined street. Finally Jack stopped and said, "Here we are." I looked up and saw that we were standing outside a big, posh house, with steps leading up to a large front door.

The music was so loud we could hear it as we walked up the stairs. I felt all buzzy and excited. Here I was, rocking up to a party in London with Jack, when a week ago I thought I was going to be stuck at home all summer. How crazy was that?

Jack opened the door for me and we walked in.

"Wow," I said. The walls were covered in paintings, there were cool-looking sculptures, and the carpet was bright red. A huge chandelier hung from the ceiling. Mum would have loved it. It was even more full of stuff than her place. I was staring at an enormous statue of a lady, when a guy walked up and bear-hugged Jack.

"Finally," he said.

"Sammy, meet Frankie," said Jack, laughing.

Sammy let go of Jack and nodded at me, flashing his bright-blue eyes. He looked nothing like Jack. Where Jack was scruffy, like most of the boys at my school, Sammy had short, neat hair and was wearing a shirt with buttons and nice pants. He was dressed more like my dad. But still, he was gorgeous. I couldn't believe how many cute boys there were in London. Maybe

Gen and I should relocate.

"You're the singer," said Sammy. "Nice work."

"Thanks," I said. "Nice party."

He laughed. "Yep, sadly that's what I'm known for."

"Actually," said Jack to me, "Sammy's a violinist, but he only plays in orchestras."

"Not true, you just haven't written me anything yet," said Sammy. "Maybe Frankie can write me a part," he said looking at me. "What do you think?"

I *think* I was blushing, because I stammered as I answered, "Um ... I'm not sure I could write a part for violin ... I don't ..."

Just then a song boomed from down the hall and Sammy grabbed both our arms, pulling us along. "Come on, I love this song!"

The living room was heaving with people dancing, but as soon as we walked in, suddenly people made space. And it didn't take me long to work out why. Sammy was a really great dancer. He used his whole body and he seemed to love it.

We weren't really dancing together, just sort of

dancing near each other. I really wished Gen could be here too. She loved dancing even more than I did, and she'd probably rival Sammy for awesome dance moves.

The music just kept coming, and half the tracks were things I'd never heard of, so Sammy promised to make me a list of stuff I had to look out for when I got home. Even though he was super cute, he somehow reminded me of one of Gen's brothers. But it was nice to make a guy friend; I felt like we could hang out without being self-conscious at all.

I wished I could feel like that about Jack. I kept trying to forget he was there, dancing close to me, but then I'd turn around and see him, arms waving, legs jumping, and remember how much I liked him all over again. He wasn't a very good dancer, but it didn't matter. I liked watching him try to keep in time with the music, his hair flopping down over his eyes.

Then someone crashed into Jack and he bumped into me, sending me flying. "Sorry, Frank," said Jack. He instinctively grabbed my arm and pulled me up before I hit the ground. As I stood up, we were suddenly squashed together by all the people dancing around us. His brown eyes found mine and it was like everything stopped.

I'm not sure what would have happened if Sammy hadn't danced right through the middle of us and split us apart. Would we have kissed?

It was a bit weird for a minute and then, because Sammy was bouncing around dancing, both Jack and I started up again.

I realized I hadn't seen Asha at the party and I asked Jack where she was. He said she'd messaged him to say she was going home. The weird thing was he didn't look upset about it, even though it was their big gig and his girlfriend had just gone home and then sent him a text. I wondered if she really had gone home or if she was with the drummer.

Just then one of my favorite songs came on so I stopped thinking about Asha and started singing at the top of my lungs. I knew all the words because Gen and I had listened to it a million times in her room.

"I said, everything you know is just a dream.

Everyone you know is gonna screeee-am!"

Jack and I were yelling in each other's faces and laughing. Sammy was dancing, and he grabbed me and twirled me around and around. I started doing the moves that Gen and I always did to this song, and Sammy picked it up pretty quickly. Jack was struggling a bit and he looked a bit put out when Sammy pulled me into the middle of the group to dance with him.

As the song finished, Jack came up and touched my arm. "We should go, Frank," he said.

Sammy heard him and held on to me. "No! She's the best dancer here. You can't leave."

I laughed. But I knew Jack was right. Mum might have agreed to me coming to the party but I'm sure she wouldn't be that happy if I missed our curfew.

When we walked out of Sammy's house, it was raining heavily. We pulled on our jacket hoods and ran towards Jack's house, laughing as we raced through the streets.

Lucky it wasn't far to his house, because the rain seemed to be coming at us horizontally. We tried to be quiet as we burst in through the front door. I kicked off my wet Converse and Jack took off his coat.

"Top night, Frank," said Jack as he gave me a big hug.

"I'll say," I said, feeling a bit weird hugging him. We were both really wet and I could feel his ribs and back through his clothes.

He held on to me a bit longer than he should have and then, as he let go, he smiled. "Thanks for being here," he said.

I didn't trust myself to speak so I just nodded. The house was so quiet and it just felt too close. I let Jack go, and started up the stairs. I wanted to get away from him – I just didn't know how to be around him tonight.

Mum woke me up in the morning with a hot chocolate and some toast. She had to go and meet with the organizers of the award so they could talk through all the details. I was pretty happy to stay in bed, but soon after she left, Jack knocked on the door.

Great. I was in stripy pajamas and had crazy morning hair.

Jack came in all dressed and looking hot, even after having no sleep. "You gotta get up. We're going to be late," he said.

I groaned. "What for?"

He smiled. "I won us tickets to see *Jaws of Death*."

"Really? Oh wow, I'm dying to see it." I loved horror films. Especially ones that were so bad they were good. And so did Jack. We'd stayed up late one night watching *Night of the Living Dead* when he stayed with us. "Twenty minutes," I said, getting up, and wondering how I was going to get ready so fast.

"You've got five," said Jack as he closed the door.

Five! It takes me so much longer than that just to wake up.

I grabbed the clothes I'd worn yesterday. Jeans, red sweater, and my very wet purple Converse. I didn't have any other shoes so they'd have to do.

I dressed in three minutes with two left to fix my wild and crazy hair. One look and I gave up. It was definitely a ponytail day.

I ran down the stairs with a minute to spare.

The cinema was huge, and packed. We had 3-D glasses on and massive boxes of popcorn, and I was sharing an armrest with Jack. I knew that I shouldn't be so excited about sitting so close to him – he had a girlfriend. But I'd decided that I wasn't going to think about Asha and Jack today. I was just going to hang out and enjoy myself. We settled down in our seats as the opening credits started.

At one point in the movie, when someone was about to be found by the guy with a rather large ax, Jack grabbed my arm, and I almost screamed. *Did he do that on purpose?* I couldn't quite relax with his hand on my arm and I moved away.

As the credits rolled, we got up and walked out into the foyer. "Awesome, wasn't it?" said Jack. "That bit where she was hiding."

"I know. Terrifying," I said.

"Come on. I'm starving," said Jack, even though he'd eaten all of his popcorn and half of mine.

It's usually really strange coming out of a cinema during the day because it's so sunny. Not in London. It was gray and dark outside and even though it was only lunchtime it felt really late.

"Are you hungry?" asked Jack. "I was thinking maybe we could head over to the East End, check out Spitalfields Markets and go to Brick Lane for lunch. Sound good?"

I nodded. "Yeah. Sure." I'd never heard of the places he was talking about, and I was a bit surprised he wanted to hang out for the whole day, but it sounded good to me.

We caught a bus to the East End instead of the tube so Jack could point out famous buildings, statues, monuments and shops on the way. I realized I'd barely seen a dot of London so far – it was so huge and busy. I loved being among it all, and recognizing famous street names from playing Monopoly at home. After a while I gave up trying to be cool about it. I was just really excited.

Eventually we jumped off the bus and Jack led me to Brick Lane, a street lined with curry houses, where spices hung in the air and the street signs were written in Bengali as well as English. Jack pulled me into one of the restaurants and pounced on two stools as people got up to leave so we were soon sitting down, squashed tightly together.

"So this place does really amazing curry and it's cheap and yum," explained Jack. "Sometimes there's a line down the street," he added.

When I go out for lunch at home it's usually just for burgers, not curry. I hoped that I'd like the food, given that Jack was so keen for me to try it.

"I'll just order some stuff to share," said Jack as he got up to go to the counter. While I waited, I looked around at all the interesting people there. There was a guy with a red Mohawk. A mum and a little boy. A really old lady perched on the edge of a stool. People on lunch breaks and people alone.

Soon an enormous plate of food appeared. I couldn't quite work out what was what. There were heaps of pappadams and curries and relishes and pickles and it all just looked amazing and a bit overwhelming. Jack wasn't waiting for me to start. He was hoeing in. I was a bit tentative at first but it was so delicious that it didn't take me long until I was eating as fast as Jack.

Some of it was a bit spicier than I was used to, but I drank the yogurt drink that Jack had bought and it seemed to cool my mouth down.

"Yum," I said, with a mouthful.

Jack smiled as he wiped the naan bread across the plate, mopping up the food. "Yep."

Jack's phone rang and he pulled it out, but didn't answer it.

"It's just Asha," he said, and he tucked his phone away. A few seconds later, I heard the buzz that meant she'd left a message. I wondered why he hadn't answered it, and what she'd said.

"How great was that gig?" asked Jack, with a mouthful of rice.

"Pretty great," I said.

"I can't believe we have a permanent spot," said Jack,

his eyes shining. "Maybe you can sing again next week."

"If you like," I said, feeling all messed up. It was like Jack was pretending he didn't have a girlfriend. But he did.

We finished our lunch and walked outside. And just as we did, it started pouring again. Jack grabbed my hand and we ran for cover, squashing up under the tiny awning of a shop. I was soaked. My hair was all wet and sticking to my face. I was super aware of how close Jack was. It made me feel crazy. I knew I was falling for him and I didn't know what to do about it.

"Frankie," said Jack, looking down at me with those soft brown eyes.

"Yeah?" I said, my heart pounding so fast I was sure Jack could hear it.

He reached down and brushed away the wet hair from my eyes. And I knew what was going to happen.

He was leaning over to kiss me and I knew that if his lips touched mine I'd kiss him back.

But he had a girlfriend and even if *he* didn't care about that, I did. It wasn't right, even if she was cheating on him. I couldn't kiss him while he was with Asha. Could I?

I really wanted to. I'd wanted to kiss him since the moment I'd arrived. And now I could.

I didn't know what to do. Should I kiss him or not?

If you think Frankie should kiss Jack, go to page 212.

If you don't think Frankie should kiss Jack, go to page 221.

Frankie GOES TO
the party

Chapter Four

"Okay, let's do it," I said finally.

"You won't regret this!" said Ellie, and she hugged me as if I were her closest friend in the world.

It was way too easy to slip out of our room through the sliding doors, jump down from the balcony and disappear into the trees. Sadly, the fact that it was so easy didn't make me feel any less guilty, and I really hoped Dad wouldn't find out. I could only imagine how long I'd be grounded for if he did, and it was a pretty scary thought. But he and Jan were watching a DVD and Ellie had given them some excuse about why we weren't joining them, and I was only going out for an hour.

Then I'd sneak back, with or without Ellie, and all would be fine (fingers crossed).

As we walked up the road to Luke and Sarah's house, I must have tugged at my dress about twenty times. Ellie finally asked, "Are you okay?"

"I never wear dresses. It just feels weird," I tried to explain.

"You don't look weird," she said. "You look good, actually."

"Thanks," I said. But I got the feeling she was just being nice because I'd sneaked out with her.

"Here we are," said Ellie. We were outside an amazing-looking house.

I was still half expecting Dad to chase me down the street and drag me back home, so I was relieved we'd made it.

It wasn't like a normal beach house. It was on three levels and there were kids spilling out onto all the balconies and the lawn. It was the perfect warm summer night for a party and we could hear the music before we even got to the front door. Ellie stopped to chat to someone, but I kept going. If I was only going to be here for an hour then I wanted to at least have a dance and see Luke and Sarah.

The door was open so I walked in. The house was even more impressive inside. It seemed to be all glass and slate floors with huge paintings on the walls. It was pretty wild being at a party and not really knowing anyone.

"Finally," said a voice.

I spun around and saw Luke. "Hi," I said.

"Nice dress," he said.

"Thanks." I suddenly felt a bit shy wearing Ellie's dress, and added, "Nice, um, shorts."

Luke laughed as he looked down at what he was wearing – shorts, a T-shirt and flip-flops. "My usual," he said.

"Well, I've never seen you in clothes before," I said, smiling. I'd only ever seen Luke barefoot and in a wetsuit on the beach.

"I dressed up for you, Frankie," he said, grinning at me.

As guilty as I felt about sneaking out, Luke's sparkling

blue eyes were definitely helping to make me feel like it was worth it. My thoughts wandered briefly back to Tom Matthews from school. He'd certainly never commented on what I was wearing. Although I guess it was usually my school uniform.

"It's an amazing house," I said, still looking around. It sort of reminded me of some of the places Mum's firm had designed. All sharp edges and lots of windows.

Luke nodded. "Yeah, perfect for a party!"

"There are so many people here," I said.

"Yep. And no parents."

That was kind of obvious. I couldn't imagine anyone's parents letting this many kids into their house. "Where are they?"

"At some function thing at the surf club with my brothers. They'll be back later, so hopefully it won't get too out of control!"

"Bit late for that!" said Ellie as she walked up. "There's, like, nearly a hundred people here."

"Whoops!" said Luke grinning.

"Where's Richie?" asked Ellie, in a voice that made

me think I was probably right about her liking him.

Luke shrugged. "Who knows?"

Someone must have changed the music because suddenly a song came on that made half the room cheer.

"I love this song! Come on," said Ellie as she grabbed Luke and me and pulled us out to one of the balconies where people were dancing.

I'd never danced outside on a huge balcony before. Through the trees I could just make out the sea. The sky was perfectly clear and I couldn't get over all the stars. Luke grabbed my hand and spun me around, and I came back to earth and grinned at him.

Ellie was dancing with us too. She squeezed my hand. "Thanks for coming, Frankie," she yelled over the music.

I smiled at her and she smiled back and it seemed like we might actually make it over the friend line.

A different song came on and Luke got pulled away by some of his friends but Ellie and I kept dancing together. She was pretty good and it was almost like messing around with Gen except that Ellie and I didn't know the same routines.

We watched Luke from a distance for a while, then she whispered in my ear, "You like him, don't you?"

I still wasn't that comfortable talking about boys with Ellie, so I sort of shrugged and smiled, and kept dancing.

She grinned. "Thought so," she said loudly over the music.

I spotted Richie dancing and pointed him out to Ellie. She dragged me towards him, but when we got closer, we saw he was dancing with a girl.

Ellie stopped and turned around, facing away from him.

"Are you okay?" I asked her, assuming she was upset.

"Just thirsty," she said, and she disappeared inside. I wished she'd just asked me to go with her because I didn't know if I should follow her or wait for her to come back. I decided to follow her. The problem was that the house was huge and she had a head start.

For the next half hour, I checked room after room and I couldn't find Ellie anywhere. Finally I found Sarah.

"Hey, Frankie, you made it," she said.

"Seems like half the town is here," I said, smiling at her.

"Yep. That's Luke's fault!" she said, laughing.

"Have you seen Ellie anywhere?" I asked.

"She was outside before," said Sarah, pointing to the garden out in front.

I walked through the big sliding glass doors and found more people. I couldn't believe Luke had invited so many kids. My parents would ground me until I was ninety just for thinking about throwing a party that big.

I saw Ellie and Richie talking under a tree and I didn't know whether to go up or not. If I was right and she did like him then she probably wouldn't thank me for interfering.

Before I could make up my mind, someone slipped their hands around my waist and spun me around to face them. Luke.

"Hi," he said. "I've been looking for you."

"Really?" I asked, smiling.

He nodded. "Yep. And now I've found you."

"You have," I said, enjoying flirting with him. He was so cute that I couldn't believe he was holding on to me.

"Want to come for a walk?" he asked.

"You can't leave your own party," I said.

"Why not? There's an awesome view down the hill. You can see the waves. That's where I check the surf in the morning. Come on," said Luke, taking my hand. He started pulling me gently down the hill, and I would have kept going with him, but then I noticed Ellie was standing under the tree on her own and she seemed to be crying. I didn't see Richie anywhere, so I could only guess he'd upset her.

"Hang on a minute, Luke. I'll just see if Ellie's okay," I said, as I walked over.

"Ellie?" I said, slipping my arm around her shoulders. Her makeup was all smudged and she was crying.

"You all right?" I asked.

"No," she said, sniffling.

I waited for her to tell me what had happened but she didn't say anything. "What's wrong?" I asked, hoping she'd start talking. "Is it Richie?"

I think she was just about to tell me when Luke walked towards us. When she saw him coming our way, she started wiping her eyes. Maybe she was embarrassed, but somehow she just changed completely. It was like she'd never been upset. She turned me towards Luke.

"Isn't she cute?" she said to him.

"Sure is," said Luke. I couldn't help but smile at him. No matter what Ellie was up to, Luke was still right there, as gorgeous as ever.

"We could end up sisters. How weird is that?" said Ellie, more to Luke than to me.

"Our parents have been dating for, like, a month." I knew I sounded angry, but I didn't get Ellie. One minute she was all friendly and sweet and the next she seemed to be trying to make me feel bad.

"Come and dance, Luke," she said, ignoring me. She grabbed his arm and pulled him back up towards the house, leaving me behind. I followed them inside and Luke shrugged at me like he didn't know what was going on either. I figured it was the end of our romantic walk.

On the dance floor, Ellie hurled herself at Luke, grabbing him around the waist and pulling him close. I didn't know what to do. Did she like him? Maybe I had it all wrong and it wasn't Richie she liked, but Luke. Maybe she just wanted me out of the way.

I backed away, not wanting to get involved in whatever was going on. If Luke liked me then he could come and find me. I wasn't going to try to compete for a boy.

I watched as Ellie grabbed Luke's hands and pulled him over to where Richie was dancing with the girl from before. The four of them started laughing and messing around and I felt really left out. What had gone wrong? One minute I was being led down the hill to look at waves and the next I was leaning against a wall, watching the boy I liked dance with the girl I was sharing a room with.

"Is that Ellie?" said Sarah, walking up to me. "With Luke?" she added. Ellie was now reaching her arms around Luke's waist and pulling him close.

"Um, yeah," I said, hurt.

"Weird," said Sarah, sounding as confused as I was.

"Yep." I turned away from them. I really didn't want to see them kiss. It was bad enough just knowing it was going to happen.

"Come on, Frankie, let's go downstairs," said Sarah, linking her arm through mine.

"Actually, I'm just going to go. I sneaked out of the house and if Dad finds out I'll be grounded forever." Then, before she could say anything, I said good-bye and quickly walked away. I wasn't sure if I felt sick, or angry, or upset. It was all a big jumble. I just wished I'd never even gone to the stupid party.

My heart was racing as I dodged through the trees back to the house. I didn't know if I would recognize the house. It was pretty dark now — even though it was a clear night, the trees were huge and they were blocking out most of the moonlight. I must have clipped a branch or something because I tripped and hit the ground hard. As I stood up, my right knee really hurt. I hoped

I hadn't scraped it.

The scene of Ellie and Luke dancing close on the dance floor kept looping over and over in my mind. I knew Ellie and I had just met, and I didn't know Luke very well either, but I'd really thought tonight was going to turn out very differently. How was I going to spend the rest of the vacation sharing a room with Ellie after this?

I wished I'd gone to London instead.

Finally I saw the hammock and I knew I was in the right place. I moved as quickly as I could along the side of the house. Even though I knew Dad and Jan were probably still watching their movie, I was worried that one of them would just look outside into the garden and see me. Sneaking out was definitely not my thing.

I held my breath and reached up for the edge of the balcony. It was much harder pulling myself up than it had been getting down. I wriggled under the metal railing and crept across to the sliding door. Now I just had to hope their movie was loud enough that they wouldn't hear the door opening.

I opened it just enough to squeeze through and then shut it again. Inside the room, I realized I was still holding my breath and I relaxed. I was safe.

I quickly took off Ellie's dress and changed into an old tank top and shorts. If Dad did come down to say good night at least it wouldn't look like I was all dressed up. In the bathroom I checked my knee. The skin was scraped and it was a bit bloody. I wet some toilet paper in the sink and wiped off the blood and dirt, hoping Dad wouldn't notice in the morning.

I climbed into bed and started thinking about everything that had happened at the party. Now that I'd had a bit more time for it to sink in, I was furious with Ellie. Why would she make me sneak out if she was just going to embarrass me by kissing Luke? And why hadn't she just told me she liked him? I was pretty sure that Luke liked me, but maybe he'd just given up on me when Ellie had thrown herself at him instead.

I knew I was going to lie awake for hours just going over and over it all in my head, so I pulled out my phone and messaged Gen.

You awake? Party crisis!

If she was still up at least I could have a cry on the phone to her about it all, and she'd probably make me laugh and feel better. But I waited ages and she didn't reply, which meant she was asleep. Gen always messaged me straight back if she knew I needed her.

I really wanted to be awake when Ellie sneaked in because I wanted to call her on what had happened, but in the end I fell asleep.

Dad and Jan were having breakfast outside in the sunshine, and I made a cup of tea and went out to join them. I felt sick seeing Dad, because the first thing he asked me was what had happened to my knee.

I looked down at the crusted blood, furious at myself for not putting on pants. "I fell over yesterday," I said vaguely. It wasn't a lie, just an omission of facts.

"Silly duffer," said Dad, and I felt weirdly disappointed that he didn't question me further. A part of me wished he could *tell* I was lying, because at least then I'd know he cared enough to be taking notice.

"Sit down, honey, and I'll get you some brekkie," said Dad kindly.

Jan was reading the paper but she stopped and looked up when I sat down. "Is Ellie still asleep?" she asked me.

I nodded.

"That girl. She could sleep forever," said Jan. "So what's the plan for you girls today?"

Great. Obviously Jan and Dad weren't intending on hanging out with us and we'd be stuck with each other again.

"I don't know," I said, sounding quite grumpy.

Dad slid two slices of toast and jam in front of me. Usually when Dad got me breakfast it was cereal. Jam was reserved for special breakfasts or when I was sick.

"Thanks, Dad," I said.

As he sat down he smiled at me. "That party went late," he said.

I looked up quickly. Did he know? I felt panicked for a second, but then I realized the comment wasn't even directed at me.

"The music didn't stop until after two," said Jan.

As they talked about it I tried to eat, but the whole idea of Dad being so nice when I'd sneaked out made me feel a bit sick.

"I'm really sorry that you didn't get to go, honey," said Dad. "I'm proud you were so good about it. Maybe we can do something special today instead."

"Yes, I suspect Ellie's probably still sulking," said Jan.

I don't know why I felt so cross about Jan's comment, maybe it was because it just highlighted how little she knew her daughter, but I hated lying to Dad. I didn't want us to be like Jan and Ellie. Dad and I had always had a really good relationship. He'd only started hiding things from me since he'd started dating Jan. And I realized that now I was doing exactly the same thing to him – I'd hidden the fact that I'd gone to the party, and been vague about how I hurt my knee. It wasn't a blatant lie, but I certainly hadn't told him the truth.

If I wanted him to be honest with me, maybe I needed to let him know the whole truth. I knew he'd be angry when he found out that I'd sneaked out behind his back, but at least I wouldn't be hiding anything from him anymore. And maybe it would show him just how preoccupied he was these days — he was so busy with his girlfriend that he didn't even notice when his own daughter went missing at night. That wasn't like him.

But if I did tell him about going to the party, I'd be getting Ellie into trouble too. She'd probably think I'd told on her just to get back at her for kissing Luke. Things were already rocky between us. I didn't want to make them worse. What if we did end up sisters one day?

I didn't know what to do. Should I tell Dad that I'd sneaked out or not?

If you think Frankie should tell her dad the truth, go to page 230.

If you think Frankie should keep quiet, go to page 239.

172

Frankie DOESN'T GO to the party

Chapter Four

"I'm sorry, Ellie. I really want to go, but if Dad found out, I'd be grounded for the rest of my life," I said sadly.

"Okay, suit yourself," said Ellie, heading towards the sliding door.

"What am I going to tell Dad and Jan if they come down and want to say good night to you?" I asked, suddenly panicked.

Ellie sighed. "Just make something up. Say I'm not feeling well, and keep them out of the room." She slid open the door onto our balcony and disappeared into the night.

It was obvious she was annoyed with me for being

such a Goody Two-shoes, but I hoped she'd get over it. The rest of the vacation would be pretty hard if she wasn't talking to me. Especially if Dad and Jan kept hanging out on their own.

Feeling lonely, I called Gen. She answered on the first ring.

"Hey, Frank! I was just thinking about you," she said.

"Is there any way you can come and rescue me?" I said dramatically.

"Why? What's happened?"

"Ellie just sneaked out to a party. She wanted me to go too but I was too scared Dad would bust me. And …" I started to say.

"You hate lying to your dad," finished Gen.

"Yeah, although he's stretched the truth a bit himself lately. So now I have to lie for Ellie if Dad or Jan come and knock on our door."

"Well, my little cousin just swiped my diary and started reading all about Arlo."

"What!?"

"Yep. Then she sat at dinner and teased me about him.

I'm going to kill her, Frankie. This vacation is painful."

"This has to be the last vacation we ever spend apart."

"Deal."

Then, before I could tell her about Luke, there was a knock on the bedroom door.

I whispered down the phone. "Someone's knocking."

"Just tell them Ellie's asleep. Sunstroke. A jellyfish sting. Or a bad ice cream. Whatevs! She's sick!"

I giggled. "Better go."

There was another knock and I really hoped it was Dad because he probably wouldn't insist on seeing Ellie. I turned off the lights in the bedroom so it looked dark and opened the door just enough to see who it was.

"Do you and Ellie fancy walking into town and getting an ice cream?" asked Dad.

I had to stop myself from laughing, thinking about Gen's advice.

"Oh, Ellie's asleep. She wasn't feeling well," I said, hoping I sounded convincing. Sometimes vague is better than too many details.

"Is she?" asked Dad. For a moment I was worried that he'd want to come in and check on her. But then he said, "Well, do you want to come?"

Relieved, I grinned and said, "Sure. I'll just grab my flip-flops."

I felt bad lying to him about Ellie, especially after our conversation about telling the truth. But I didn't really have a choice. Besides it wasn't like *I'd* sneaked out. I shut the bedroom door and followed Dad out.

"Thought you deserved a treat, given you were so good about missing out on the party," said Dad.

As much as I wanted to see Luke again, going for a walk with just Dad was a pretty good second, and it made me feel like I'd made the right decision not to sneak out with Ellie. It was the first time I'd spent alone with him since we got here. Maybe I'd finally get a chance to tell him I was feeling a bit left out. At the very least, I'd get a double cone of chocolate and strawberry ice cream.

But as Dad and I started down the steps, Jan called

out, "Wait for me!"

Of course she wouldn't let us go without her. Great. This *so* wasn't what I had in mind.

"Where's El?" she asked as she caught up with us and slipped her arm through Dad's.

"Asleep," I said, not caring if I lied to her at all.

"At nine o'clock! Are you sure?" she said, stopping on the stairs like she was going to head back in and check.

"She's not feeling well," said Dad. This seemed to satisfy Jan and they started down the street towards the beach.

"She's probably sulking about the party," said Jan. "She's having a bit of trouble adjusting to all these new rules."

Actually, she's just ignoring them completely, I felt like saying. But I didn't. I just trudged along behind them, not really saying anything.

As we walked down onto the street, we must have been getting closer to the party because we could hear the music. I couldn't believe I was now going for a romantic night walk with Dad and his girlfriend while every other teenager in the place was at Luke's party. How tragic could it get? I wondered if Ellie was having a good time, and if Luke was sorry I didn't come. Now that Jan was with us, I really wished I had sneaked out with Ellie. Even if I had been caught.

When we came to the beach, Dad and I stopped to kick off our flip-flops. He pushed them down into the sand so just the toes were peeping out.

Jan must have seen us, because she said, "What are you doing?"

"Leaving our flip-flops," said Dad, as if it were the most normal thing in the world. It was to us.

"Don't do that," she said. "They might get stolen."

I laughed. "Why would anyone want to steal two pairs of manky old flip-flops?"

But clearly Jan was serious. "John, please," she said to Dad. I hadn't really heard her use this tone before, like she was quietly making her point known. And I couldn't believe it when Dad actually picked up the flip-flops. Both pairs of them!

"Here you go, kiddo," he said, holding mine out. "Jan's probably right."

I didn't care if Jan was right. I didn't care if my flip-flops got stolen. I cared about the fact that Dad had just let her boss him around. I snatched them from him and threw them back near the path.

"Frankie," said Dad sharply.

"They're *my* flip-flops," I said, walking off down the beach, furious with Dad.

As if it wasn't bad enough having Jan crash my beach walk with Dad, now she was telling me what to do like she was my mum. And the worst thing was that Dad was letting her do it.

If I hadn't been in such a bad mood, I would have loved walking along the beach. It was a clear night, the stars were out and the air was warm. Dad and I always went for night walks. It was the thing we did in the summer when we couldn't sleep. We wouldn't talk much, just walk our way around the streets, or along the beach if we were on vacation. But with Jan clutching Dad's hand the whole time, I didn't want to walk near them. Instead I traced along the edge of the water, my feet sinking in the cool wet sand. I looked up at the stars and thought about Mum, on the other side of the planet. I wished I could be there with her instead of here with Dad and Jan.

By the time we got to the little row of shops, the ice cream place was closing up. I watched the man dragging in the tables and chairs from outside, and folding up the umbrellas, and I knew we were too late. Jan just shrugged like it didn't matter, but Dad took one look at my face, and ran across the road to the shop.

"John, we've got ice cream in the freezer," Jan called after him.

I waited for Dad to turn around and walk back, but this time he didn't. This time he ignored her and went up to the man in the shop. He must have done some fast talking because the next thing I knew a giant ice cream was being placed in my hand.

"Thanks, Dad." I gave it a big lick, then held it out to him for a taste. He never bought himself an ice cream, but the deal was that he could always try mine.

"Strawberry's good," he said. "It's always better in a cone, Jan."

For some reason, Dad buying the ice cream made all the difference to my mood, like he was his old self again. We started back along the beach, and this time Jan was behind us. Dad pointed out some of the constellations like he always did, and started singing snatches of a song he knew about a starry night on the beach. Dad and I had really similar music tastes. We liked playing guitar together and often swapped old vinyl we'd bought. We launched into a conversation about music then and I was having such a good time I'd almost forgotten that Jan was with us. But after a few minutes, she called out, "Hey, you two, wait for me."

I was halfway through saying something, but Dad just spun around and walked back to her. "Come on, slow coach," I heard him say. It was so annoying, the way he ditched me in the middle of a conversation to go running back to her. Maybe Ellie was right after all about him not having time for me now that he was with her mum.

At the entrance to the beach, I made a big deal of

finding my flip-flops right where I'd thrown them, and then stalked off towards the house, with Dad and Jan behind me. I decided to pin Dad down about surf lessons before we got home. If I was going to be ignored by Ellie and left by myself, I wanted to at least get something out of the rest of the vacation.

I turned around to face them. "Dad, can you sort out the surf lessons tomorrow?" I asked.

"Sure, honey," said Dad with a smile.

"Actually, John," said Jan. "I think we should look into it a bit more. A girl drowned at one of those surf schools last year."

I waited at least three seconds for Dad to say something, but when it was clear he had no idea how to answer her, I couldn't help myself.

"No offense, Jan, but it's nothing to do with you," I said, steaming.

"Frankie, that's enough," said Dad.

Jan didn't have to say anything because Dad had just taken her side, and made it very clear where his loyalties were. I raced off, flip-flops in hand, my feet hating the rough ground. I wished, for the second time that night, that there was some way I could still catch a plane to London and escape this horrible vacation.

"You missed a top party," said Ellie the next morning.

"I told them you were sick," I said.

"Ta," she said as she walked into the bathroom and shut the door.

I don't know why I bothered covering for her if she didn't even appreciate it. I lay on my bed counting my new freckles because I didn't want to face Jan, but after a while I was so hungry that I knew I couldn't hold out much longer. I'd have to make a run for the kitchen and hope Jan wasn't there.

But it was Dad who was making coffee when I walked into the kitchen. He gave me a smile and I thought for a second all would be forgotten. No such luck.

"Frankie, about last night. You can't speak to Jan like that. This is her house and you're a guest. I expect you to apologize," he said firmly.

I frowned. I had been rude to her, but only because Dad hadn't stood up to her. He was my dad. Surely it was up to him whether I did surfing lessons, not Jan.

"I know all this is hard, and that we're all just working it out as it comes but you have to be a bit more understanding," he said.

I really didn't know what to say. He'd already hurt me by siding with Jan, but this was even worse. He really expected me to put up with whatever she threw at me.

"Fine. I'll apologize," I said, feeling disappointed in myself. "But, Dad, you have to see that she has no right to tell me what to do. She's not my mum. She hardly knows me. I'm only here because you guys invited me. Partly I think to hang out with Ellie so you two could go off and have fun without feeling guilty."

There. I'd said it. By the look on Dad's face, I might have just upset him quite a bit, but he'd upset me, too, and he was the grown-up, after all.

"Aw, Frankie. Is that really how you feel?" asked Dad.

"Yeah. She kept telling me what to do last night. And telling you what to do. Since when did anyone tell *you* what to do?" I asked, sort of wishing I could stop talking because I sensed it was making it worse.

"Sorry, kiddo. I had no idea you felt like that," said Dad.

"Well, I do," I said, sounding like a spoiled little kid. "You promised I could have surf lessons," I added. "I know you have strict rules about things like parties, but you usually let me do sports! You said I could learn to surf on this vacation. It was the whole reason I agreed to come."

"Actually, maybe Jan had a good point about that," said Dad.

I sighed, feeling cross. It didn't matter *what* I said, he'd still defend her. He must have seen I was unhappy with his answer, because he put down his cup of coffee and walked up for a big hug. I let him hug me but I didn't feel like hugging him back, even though I knew I was being childish.

"All right, I'll talk to Jan. Okay? No more going

off and leaving you and Ellie. And I'll ask her to stop telling you what to do. And me," he said.

I started to hug him. Then he added, "But I'm still not sure about the surf lessons. Okay?"

He let me go and looked me in the eyes. Then he smiled. "Okay?" he asked again.

I nodded. It *wasn't* okay. The deal on this vacation was that I'd get surf lessons. And now they were suddenly off the table. But I knew better than to argue with Dad. It wouldn't get me anywhere, and at least now I felt like he wasn't angry with me anymore.

I took my breakfast back to the bedroom and Ellie was dressed and lying on her bed texting. I didn't say anything to her, but she looked over as I started eating my toast.

"Did you make some for me?" she asked.

"No," I said.

"Meany," she said, smiling. "What are you doing today?" she asked, sitting up on her bed and tossing her phone down.

"I don't know. I was going to learn how to surf,

but ..." I trailed off, not wanting to blame her mum and make things even more awkward.

"Yeah, I heard you and your dad. Mum played the drowning-kid card, didn't she?" asked Ellie.

"How do you know?" I asked.

She shrugged. "She always goes on about that. It's just that she knew the kid's mum and it really shook her. I don't think it was anyone's fault. The kid just fell off a board and got sucked under and couldn't swim very well. But Mum is all panicky about it."

"Oh," I said, feeling slightly different about it now. It wasn't just that Jan was trying to ruin my vacation, she did actually feel worried about it.

"But I'm a good swimmer," I said. "I used to be on the swim team."

"I can talk to her for you. Explain you're a good swimmer. It's just that Mum can be really cool about some things, but then she has these rules that she won't bend. Sorry you're having such a bad time," she said.

This time I shrugged. I didn't really know what to say. "It's okay," I managed. "I guess it's just hard when there's a new parent with new rules," I said.

"Tell me about it," said Ellie. "I was so shocked when your dad said we couldn't go to the party."

"Yeah, but you went anyway, right?"

"True," admitted Ellie. "If it makes you feel any better, Luke missed you last night. He asked me about five times why you didn't come," she said, rolling her eyes. "We could hang out with those guys later if you like?"

It was nice to know that Luke noticed I wasn't there. "Did you have fun?"

She nodded. "Yeah. It was crazy. Like, over a hundred people. When his parents came home they went ballistic."

I laughed. I imagined how my parents would react if I'd invited a hundred kids to a party at home.

Ellie flicked her hair back, and I couldn't help noticing the blue earrings she was wearing. They were these balls of bright blue.

"Cool earrings," I said.

"Thanks. I got them in town yesterday," she said. "We could go and get some for you."

I smiled at the idea. "Not unless they were clip-ons!"

She made a face. "Really? No holes?" she looked so shocked that I started to laugh.

"Nope. Mum *and* Dad this time," I said.

"Why?" She got up off the bed and walked over and sat on the end of my bed. It was sort of nice. Like she was trying to be friendly.

"I don't know. They said I could do it when I was fourteen," I said.

"But isn't that soon?" she asked me.

"Yeah. Two weeks," I said, suddenly excited about the idea of turning fourteen. Mum was going to take me and Gen to Sydney for the weekend and stay in a hotel that had a pool on the roof. It was going to be very grown-up and cool.

"Well, couldn't I give you an early birthday present?" she asked with a sly look. I smiled, admiring the way Ellie thought. She was much more cunning than I was.

"Um, probably not," I said, "but thanks for the offer."

"Oh, come on, Frankie," she said. "It'll be fun! There's a shop in town that does ear-piercing. I know a girl who works there. And your dad won't care if you pierce your ears a few days early. He probably won't even notice, the studs are so tiny. And if he does, he can't do much about it then anyway. Come on. We can say we're bonding."

I couldn't believe that I was actually considering it. If Dad did notice, he wouldn't be happy about it. And neither would Mum. But I *was* turning fourteen in two weeks, and I had already missed out on the party because of Dad's rules, and now it looked like I'd miss out on surfing lessons too. Ellie was right – it would be fun, and it was nice that she wanted us to do something together.

I didn't know what to do.

If you think Frankie should get her ears pierced, go to page 248.

If you think Frankie shouldn't get her ears pierced, go to page 257.

Frankie DOESN'T talk to Jack

Chapter Five

"I'm sorry, Asha," I said. "I just don't want to get involved."

Asha's eyes flashed. "Well, maybe you should have thought about that before you stuck your nose in and told my boyfriend that I cheated on him!" she said, getting up from my bed.

"I'm sorry, Asha. I told him about that because he's my friend and I didn't want to see him get hurt."

"Whatever," she hissed. "Forget it, Frankie. I know you still have a thing for him. I won't get in the way of your stupid little romance." Then she stormed out of my bedroom.

That had all happened a week ago and since then, Jack and I had spent every minute together. He'd admitted that Asha had made him stop e-mailing me and he said he was really sorry about it.

In the last week he'd taken me around to lots of famous music sights in London, like the crosswalk where the Beatles had photographed the *Abbey Road* cover. We'd taken each other's photo standing in the middle of the road.

We'd spent hours scouring Camden Town for rare vinyl and then come home and played the records over and over again, arguing about which was the best song. But nothing had happened between us. No kisses. No hugs. We were just hanging out like friends. Maybe it was because we had music to connect us, or maybe because we were having so much fun and we didn't want to ruin anything. I didn't want things to be all messy again. Because I was going home soon, I think I just wanted to keep it simple.

We'd been rehearsing a lot too, because even though I hated the idea of being a replacement singer for Asha, I loved the idea of getting to sing a whole gig on a stage in London. And they were paying me!

Sammy had come up with a violin part for "Tomorrow Land," and it was going to sound amazing. He'd dropped around a few times to hang out, and it was fun jamming with him. There was still a little spark between us, and I could tell that Jack was a bit funny about it, which I guess meant he felt jealous. And, despite the fact I thought it was best if nothing happened between me and Jack now, I kind of liked the idea that he was jealous.

Last night was the International Architecture and Design Awards and I got to go along with Mum. I was really proud of her. She was presented with this huge gold award that looked like a large building, and she joked about it not fitting in her suitcase.

In the cab on the way home, Mum asked me what was going on with Jack now that he and Asha had broken up.

I shrugged. "Nothing much."

Mum looked closely at me. "You sure, honey?"

"Yep. I'm sure. I think it's just not the right time," I said, realizing as I did that I was telling her the truth. "Maybe next time."

"That might be sooner than you think. I was just offered a project in London, so I might be coming back for a few months. You could always come too, if you'd like," Mum said with a smile.

My heart started racing at the thought. *A few months. In London. With Jack. And the band.* I started to nod, excited, and then I started thinking about Dad and Gen, and everything at home, and I realized this decision was going to take a little longer to make.

After we got home, Mum went up to bed, but I was starving so I headed into the kitchen to find a snack. I'd assumed Jack would be asleep already, but I found him cooking bacon.

"You having breakfast now?" I asked cheekily.

He smiled. "I could eat bacon all day, Frank, you know that. Want some?"

I nodded. It beat eating peanut butter sandwiches, which was where I'd been headed.

I sat at the kitchen table and watched him. I never got tired of watching him. His skinny legs and his long arms. His jeans that always sat just below his waist. I wished I didn't still think he was so cute, but I did.

He slid a huge plate of bacon onto the table, pulled out some white bread and sat down opposite me. I looked down at it.

"What's this?" I asked, disappointed.

"Bacon sarnie," he said as he put some bacon on a piece of bread and slapped another piece of bread on top. "Try it."

I did. And it was delicious. "Yum!" I said, surprised.

Jack laughed. "See? I'm a culinary master."

"Hmm, I wouldn't go that far."

"How was your night?" asked Jack with his mouth full.

"Great. Mum was amazing. She sounded so confident," I said, remembering her speech. I'd never really seen her in that kind of way before.

"Yeah, that's where you get it from. When you sing," he said.

"You think I look confident on stage?"

Jack nodded. "Absolutely. You nail it up there. You seem totally comfortable."

"Really?" I was pleased. I loved singing, but I still felt nervous sometimes, so it was nice to think that I looked like I belonged on stage.

"You excited about tomorrow night?" said Jack. "Or do you still not want to sing any of my songs?" he asked, with a cheeky grin.

I raised an eyebrow. "I've apologized for that a hundred times already." And I had.

"Yeah. Well, I never get tired of hearing you say sorry."

"Argh, I'm sorry! I love your songs. Okay?" I said, making a silly face.

Jack smiled, looking pleased at the apology. "So are you excited about the gig?"

"Yeah," I said. "Especially 'Tomorrow Land' and Sammy. I love that violin part he wrote."

As soon as I'd said it, I realized I'd hurt Jack's feelings. I hadn't meant to, but I was just so thrilled we had added a violin part to the song. "Jack, the whole gig will be great. You know what I meant."

"Yeah, Sammy's *awesome*," he said, without looking at me.

I felt like rolling my eyes at him. "Yeah, he is," I said, because I couldn't be bothered with his feelings right now.

"Really?" asked Jack, looking up at me. I saw how serious he seemed and I knew I'd been right. He *was* jealous about Sammy and me. I didn't know if I should set him straight or just let him feel what I'd felt when he'd been with Asha.

"You've eaten all the bacon," I said, pointing to the empty plate.

"I can cook more," he said, getting up.

I laughed. "No, it's fine. I've eaten my body weight!"

Then Jack really surprised me by bursting out with, "I wish you were living here, Frank."

"Oh," I said. "Thanks."

"No, well, you know, then you could be in the band all the time," he said, blushing a bit. "We're going to have to audition for a new singer after you leave. If you were living here then it would just be easy."

The band. It was like his cover for how he felt. I could have called him on it. I could have even told him how I felt. But instead I just nodded, agreeing. "Yeah, that'd be great if I was in the band, wouldn't it?"

"I was thinking that maybe, before you go, we could record 'Tomorrow Land,'" said Jack.

"Really?" I'd love to go home with a recording.

He nodded. "Yeah. The band's up for it. And so is Sammy. We can use the studio at his posh school. What do you think?"

I was so pleased that he'd thought to ask everyone and arrange it and spring it on me like a surprise, like a present. It was a lovely idea.

"Awesome," I said. "That would be amazing."

Jack smiled at me and reached out to grab my hands. He squeezed them and gave me a silly grin. I couldn't believe how right it felt holding his hands.

"You know, Jack, I might be coming back soon," I said, causing him to look surprised. "Mum's been offered a job for a bit over here and I might come with her. What do you think?" I asked, hoping he'd say he wanted me to.

But he didn't say anything. He just looked me straight in the eyes and grinned. A massive, cute, gorgeous grin that said absolutely everything it needed to say. And then he leaned forward, and kissed me.

Suddenly, all my feelings for Jack came rushing back. My knees buckled and my heart raced. I thought that maybe the decision to come back here wouldn't be so hard after all.

The End

Frankie AGREES TO *talk to Jack*

Chapter Five

"Okay, I'll talk to him," I finally agreed.

"Really?" said Asha excitedly. "Oh wow. That's brilliant. Thanks so much."

We sat there for a moment, not saying anything.

"So, do you want to go talk to him now?" asked Asha. "I'll wait up here and see what he says."

No, I don't want to go and talk to him now! I wanted to say. I'd agreed to help Asha because I felt sorry for her, but it still wasn't easy for me to go and tell the boy I'd liked for so long that he should get back with his girlfriend.

"Maybe we should just give him a bit of time," I said, stalling. "I mean, I can talk to him, but he could still be upset about it. I don't know how he'll react." I figured it was probably best not to tell Asha that Jack was already acting like she was last week's news. "Let's leave it till later."

"You're probably right." Asha sighed. "Thanks, Frankie. Okay, I'll talk to you tomorrow."

It *was* later. Much later. Like the next day. In my defense I hadn't seen much of Jack, but I guess I was also putting it off. The last time I'd really spoken to him I'd told him I didn't want to sing his songs, so I think we'd been avoiding each other. But now I could hear Jack rattling around in the kitchen and I knew I couldn't avoid him forever. He gave me a little smile as I walked in.

"What are you up to today?" he asked.

"Haven't decided," I said coolly.

"Want to come to Camden Market with me?"

"Ah," I stalled.

"There's heaps of great vinyl," he added, knowing that would make it hard for me to resist.

I knew this would be my chance to talk to him about Asha. But I had absolutely no idea how he'd react. And even though I'd agreed to talk to him, I wasn't looking forward to it. At all.

The weird thing was that since Asha had told me that Jack had talked about me all the time, I'd been hoping something might happen, but nothing had. Maybe he was brokenhearted over Asha, but he sure didn't show it. So I'd sort of accepted that he must have been talking about me all the time as a friend – in the same way that, back home, Tom Matthews had told his girlfriend, Jasmine, about my singing. At least I had no shortage of *friends*.

"If you want to come, we should go soon. All the good stuff sells out early," said Jack.

"Okay," I said, making myself a peanut butter sandwich. "I'll just grab my stuff."

Mum had already gone out with Tina, so I left her a note telling her where I was going.

"Frankie, you ready?" Jack called up the stairs.

I took a long breath. *Not really.* "Yeah, coming," I shouted back.

Jack and I opened the door and found Sammy standing on the front step.

"Um, hi," he said, smiling nervously. "I was just about to knock."

I was really pleased to see him.

Sammy looked up at me. "I was coming to see you, Frankie. I would have sent you a text but I didn't have your number."

Jack looked a bit shocked.

"Sammy walked me home the other night," I reminded Jack, smiling a little at his surprise.

Jack nodded. "Yeah, course. After the party."

Then we all stood on the step, just looking around, nobody really knowing what to do or say, until Jack said, "Well, we're heading to Camden Market, wanna come?"

"Oh, um, no, that's okay. What about if I come by later, Frankie? I'll bring my violin," he said.

I nodded. "Yeah, that'd be great."

Sammy and Jack said good-bye and I watched Sammy walk away before realizing that Jack was looking at me strangely.

"What?" I said.

He shrugged. "Nothing. Just surprised by your new BFF."

I shrugged, wondering about his attitude. "He's nice. We talked about music."

"Uh-huh," said Jack. I knew he was feeling jealous or something like that, but actually he had no right. He'd been a bit of a pain lately, and if Asha was telling the truth he'd obviously made her feel just as jealous about me as he'd made me jealous of her. It was about time he felt it back.

The market *was* amazing. And Jack was right. There were heaps of stalls selling old vinyl. I couldn't wait to start rifling through boxes.

"This is incredible," I said, looking around and not knowing where to start.

"Yep. I really wanted to bring you here. I knew you'd love it," said Jack, his eyes smiling.

I wanted him to stop saying things like that. It just

confused me. I needed to talk to him about Asha, not get all mixed up about how he felt.

"I'll meet you back here in an hour," I said, needing to escape Jack for a bit and wander around on my own.

"Oh. Okay," said Jack, sounding surprised that I didn't want to shop with him. Then he pointed out an old fifties trailer. "Meet you near the doughnut van. We can share a bag when you've finished shopping."

As I poked around, I realized I could spend days at the market. I found something I wanted to buy at almost every stall. But I just wanted a few really special things to take home with me.

After I finally decided on which records to buy, I headed back to the doughnut van. Jack was stuffing his face, and I decided if I was going to say anything to him then now was the time.

"So, Asha came and saw me yesterday," I said.

He looked at me strangely over his bag of doughnuts. I took one, hoping the sugar would help me tell him what I'd agreed to tell him.

"Why?" he asked.

"She wants me to talk to you for her," I said, feeling stupid even saying it. "About why she kissed Sean."

"And you agreed?" he asked.

"Yeah. I did, because she said she was jealous," I said.

Jack smiled. "Of what?"

Great. Now I felt even more stupid. According to Jack, she had nothing to even feel jealous about. How did I get caught up in all of this?

"Me." *There. I'd said it.*

Jack just nodded. Took another doughnut from his bag and bit into it, sending jam dripping down his chin. He wiped it away with his hand.

"So she kissed Sean because of you," he said.

"That's what she said."

"And do you believe her?" he asked me.

I nodded. I did. It was a dumb thing to do, but I still thought she'd told me the truth.

"So, what do I do about it, Frank?" he raised an eyebrow. "Do *you* want me to get back with her?"

Suddenly spending time jamming with Sammy seemed like a much better thing to be doing than hanging out at this market. I didn't want to talk to Jack about all this. It seemed like he was just fishing for compliments, and I wasn't even sure he was taking it seriously.

"You know what, Jack? I don't care what you do. Go out with her. Or not. It's nothing to do with me," I said as I handed him half my doughnut. I didn't even like doughnuts.

"Right," he said, sounding cross.

"I'm going back to the house. I want to catch up with Sammy," I said, and walked away. Part of me was hoping Jack would chase after me and tell me Asha was right to be jealous.

I heard him call after me and I didn't turn around, so he chased after me and grabbed my arm.

"Frankie, I'm sorry," he said.

I turned around to face him. "Me too."

He looked really sad. I wondered what else he was going to say.

"You're right, I made Asha jealous and it wasn't fair. I used to talk about you all the time. When I started going out with Asha I wasn't over you."

"Oh." I was surprised at how honest he was being.

"I'll go and see her now," he said with a weak smile. "And apologize."

I was stunned. Even though I'd promised to talk to Jack, I didn't actually think it would change his mind. But then I thought about everything I'd seen him do over the past few days: the way he was with me and her, the way he'd just disappeared last time. In my heart I knew that if Jack had really liked me, he wouldn't have stopped e-mailing. And he wouldn't have started dating Asha in the first place.

"Yeah, you should go and see her," I said. I really meant it.

Jack wasn't the boy for me. I could enjoy his company and we could have fun hanging out, but he was like a gorgeous guitar that I could admire, but never really own. And that was okay.

The End

Frankie KISSES Jack

Chapter Five

I leaned up and Jack's lips touched mine. And, like that, we were kissing. He reached his arms around my waist and pulled me close. I breathed him in and held his wet back.

When we opened our eyes we both sort of jumped back from each other, like we were shocked we'd just kissed.

"Oh, Frank, I'm so sorry," he said, moving away even further. "I didn't … mean … to do that," he bumbled.

Really? Why wasn't he happy about it? I didn't know what to say. Why did he keep doing this to me?

I grabbed my bag from where it had slipped onto

the ground and rushed out into the rain. I didn't care if I got wet. I just wanted to get away from Jack as quickly as I could.

"Frankie, wait," called Jack.

I heard him calling my name, but I wouldn't stop. I kept running, dodging through all the people and umbrellas. I had no idea where I was going. It was so rainy and gray that I couldn't even really see the streets. I figured I'd try to head back to where we'd gotten off the bus, then I'd get out of the rain and work out how to get back to Jack's house.

Actually, I didn't even really want to go back. I just wanted to avoid Jack for the rest of the time I was in London.

I spotted the massive Liverpool Street station building and ran straight across the road towards it. There was tooting and yelling as I ran across the street, but I kept going until I was under cover. I needed a plan. If I could have called Gen to come and help me I would have, but I couldn't. I was cold and wet, and all alone in a massive city.

But I knew it wasn't going to do me any good to sit around feeling sorry for myself. I saw a sign for the bathrooms, and went in. I washed my face, dried off with paper towel, and pulled myself together. I was at one of London's main train stations – surely it would connect with the station near Jack's place? So with new resolve, I walked out of the bathroom, found a map of the Underground on the wall, and worked out how to get back.

It was surprisingly easy to catch the tube. Everything was so clearly signposted that even though I had to change trains a couple of times, I was back at Jack's place in an hour. But I was relieved to get there. I couldn't wait to get out of my wet clothes and have a hot chocolate.

Mum was sitting in the family room reading the paper when I walked through the front door. "Oh my goodness, look what the cat dragged in!" she laughed.

I looked at her and then, before I could stop myself, I started to cry.

"Honey? Are you okay? Where's Jack?" Mum rushed over to me and hugged me. It made me cry more.

"I'm okay. I'm just a bit cold," I managed.

"Go upstairs and have a hot shower, then we'll talk some more," Mum said firmly.

After I'd had a shower and gotten changed into dry clothes, Mum and I sat drinking hot chocolate in the kitchen and I told her everything that had happened. Not just today, but right from the start — from when he'd stayed with us in Australia, and then the way he'd cut off contact with me, and the way he'd been towards me since we'd gotten here. I told her how confused I was, how I still really liked him and I thought that he liked me, but I didn't want to get between him and Asha, even though Asha had kissed someone else.

Mum just listened and then gave me a big kiss and a hug. "Honey, sometimes everything gets a bit messed up, but I bet Jack didn't mean to hurt you," she said.

"But he did. Twice," I said, feeling really sad. "And I don't want to see him again."

"Well, you don't have much choice, Frankie. We're

not leaving for another ten days," she said. "You need to talk to him and tell him how you feel."

I knew she was right but I hated the idea of seeing him, and I really hated the idea of having to ever see Asha again. It just made me so mad that he was going out with her when he could have been going out with me.

"I don't think I can. At least, not today," I said.

She nodded. "Sometimes it's good to have a bit of time to think about these things."

Then Mum got this huge smile on her face and grabbed my hand. "Come on, I know what will cheer you up. Get your coat. We're going out."

All the way back to the house, I kept touching my ears to make sure my earrings were real. Mum was right. It *had* cheered me up, and it even made me feel a bit braver about facing Jack. If I could have studs shot through my earlobes then I could face a stupid boy who didn't know what he was missing.

Before we went inside, I said, "Mum, can you take a photo of my ears with my phone? I want to message Gen."

She laughed. "Sure, honey."

So I held up my hair and Mum snapped a couple of photos. I knew Gen would squeal when she saw them.

When we opened the front door, Jack was waiting for me in the family room. Mum gave my hand a squeeze and disappeared upstairs.

"I left about a hundred messages," he said, sounding angry. "I didn't know if you were okay."

"I'm here, aren't I?" I said, sounding as angry as I felt.

"Frankie," he said, his voice softening as he walked towards me.

"What?" I said sharply.

I expected him to get angry but instead he started to smile. I wanted to kill him. It wasn't funny. He'd really hurt me. And now he was being all cute and gorgeous.

"It's not funny!" I said, fuming.

"It is a bit," he said, as he kept getting closer.

I turned to go upstairs. I'd had enough of his games.

But before I could leave, he reached out and grabbed my hand.

"Frankie," he said, pulling me back towards him. "I went and told Asha. We've been fighting since you got here. I guess I still liked you. Anyway, I'm sorry I kissed you before I broke up with her, but it's all done now," he said quietly.

My heart was exploding. He'd broken up with her. For me!

"Really?" I asked. "You've broken up?"

He nodded and then smiled at me. That gorgeous Jack smile. And I smiled back. Neither of us said anything for a minute. Then he leaned down and kissed me again and it was even better than last time.

I could have stood there all day kissing him, but then he moved his hands across my face, and up over my ears.

"Ow!" I said, moving away.

"What, Frankie?" he said, looking worried.

Laughing at his expression, I lifted up my hair to show him my ears. "I just got my ears pierced. They still hurt!"

"Cute," he said, smiling.

I had so many questions about what would happen when I left. Would he e-mail this time? Would we Skype? Would it work, being in two different countries?

As Jack leaned down to kiss me again, I decided the questions could all wait for another day. Right now we had more than enough to do.

Frankie DOESN'T KISS Jack

Chapter Five

Before Jack could lean down to kiss me, I turned my head, grabbed my bag and marched out into the rain.

"Do you want to check out the markets next?" I said. It was pouring, but I wasn't going to stand under that awning with Jack and let him kiss me while he still had a girlfriend. That was just going to end badly for me. And I really didn't want to go home heartbroken. Not after how long it had taken me to get over him last time.

Jack caught up with me. "Um, Frankie, you're going the wrong way."

I had no idea where I was going, I was just walking. Trying to get away from the moment.

"It's this way," he said.

I followed Jack back in the other direction, neither of us talking. Jack's phone started ringing and, as he pulled it out, I knew it would be Asha calling. He looked at the phone and then at me.

"Aren't you going to answer it?" I asked.

"Um," he stalled.

I was so embarrassed that I just wanted the ground to swallow me up. In fact, the idea of having to spend the rest of the day hanging out with him was more than I could deal with.

"Actually, Jack, I don't feel so well," I said, lying. "I think I'm just going to head home."

He nodded as his phone beeped. Possibly as relieved as I was that this whole awkward moment was vanishing. "Do you know how to get home?" he asked.

"I'll find it. ' I said. "Would it be quicker to catch the tube than a bus?"

"Yeah. You know where we got off the bus at Liverpool Street station? You can catch the tube from there." He pulled a small map of the Underground out of his wallet and showed me where I needed to change and where to get out. "It's pretty straightforward."

I actually didn't care if I ended up on the moon. As long as I didn't have to be there with Jack.

"Okay. See ya." I didn't wait for him to say good-bye. I just spun around and started walking.

I was so mad at him. He would have kissed me, and then what would have happened? I would have been pretending it hadn't happened for the rest of the vacation. He was no better than Asha. In fact they were a good pair. They could cheat on each other happily for the rest of their lives. As long as they both stayed away from me.

Liverpool Street station was enormous and had some cool little shops that I knew Gen would have loved, so I bought a few things for her and that made me feel better. I stocked up on buttons, new notebooks and pencils, and some cool nail polish.

By the time I found my way home, I'd decided I didn't want to be around Jack at all. And I had a plan that I hoped Mum might understand.

She was trying on her gorgeous new dress for the awards night when I found her.

"You look great," I said, smiling at the sight. And she did. It really suited her.

"I'm a bit nervous, Frankie. About tonight. I don't like making speeches," she said.

I totally understood that. Singing was fine because it was the thing I knew I was good at, but I wasn't a fan of public speaking either.

"You'll be fine, Mum," I said. I was actually really excited about seeing Mum accept the design award. So excited that for a second I almost forgot what I'd wanted to talk to her about. Almost, but not quite. "So, I saw an ad at the tube station," I said, changing tack.

"Mmm?" she said, sounding like her thoughts were somewhere else.

"An ad for the Eurostar. Did you know that Paris is less than three hours from London?"

She stopped looking at herself in the mirror and turned towards me. Even though she could be vague when she was thinking about work, she was so good at knowing when I was about to say something important. "Is that right?" she smiled.

"Yes. Do you think we could go? It's not far. And we could eat cheese. And baguettes. It would be amazing," I said, knowing it was probably sounding crazy. And by the look on Mum's face, I was right.

"Where's all this coming from?" she asked. "I thought you liked London."

Should I tell her the truth? Or just try to fudge it past her? That didn't usually work so I took a big breath. "I do, but I'd kind of like to get away from Jack for a few days."

"Is everything okay?" she asked. She had her Worried Mum face on.

"Yes. But it's pretty full-on staying here, and I just need a break," I said, hoping she'd stop at that.

Surprisingly, Mum didn't push it. Instead she got this dreamy look on her face and sighed. "It would be lovely, wouldn't it? A girls' trip to Paris?"

"Yeah," I said enthusiastically.

"If we went tomorrow ..."

"What?" I couldn't believe my ears.

"Well ... I'm just thinking. It could only be for a few days. I've got a meeting in the London office at the end of the week. But I could do some preparation for it while we're in Paris. And I could fit that in around some sightseeing. As long as you don't mind hanging out with your boring old mum," she said, smiling.

"Are you kidding? That would be awesome!" I said. I couldn't think of anyone I'd rather be in Paris with. I know it was supposed to be a romantic city, but romance was overrated. This was a chance to travel and see an amazing new city.

Mum smiled. "My French is a bit rusty, so you might need to help me out."

Her French was rusty! I may have "studied" French at school, but it seemed we mainly practiced ordering coffee with milk. As long as all Mum wanted was a *café au lait*, we'd be fine. But I decided now was not the time to reveal this piece of information.

"Of course! It'd be great to practice my French!" I said.

"Okay. Why not?" she said.

I grinned. Mum was the best.

"On one condition, Frankie," she added.

"Yeah?"

"You tell me what really happened with Jack when we're on the train," she said, smiling.

"Deal."

Actually, I was looking forward to having a real chat with Mum and hearing what she had to say about everything that had happened with Jack. Maybe I was crazy not to kiss him today, when I still liked him so much, but if he was with Asha, it just didn't seem fair – to her, or to me. When I really fell for someone, it wouldn't be someone who had a girlfriend. It would be someone who liked me as much as I liked him.

And at least this way I was going to get to eat croissants, see the Eiffel Tower, and have an amazing time in Paris with my mum – boys may come and go, but you only get one mum, and I knew she'd always be there for me, no matter what. Besides, from what I'd heard, French boys could be pretty cute. At least as cute as English ones.

Frankie TELLS HER DAD *the truth*

Chapter Five

I took a huge breath and then said, "Actually, Dad. I did go to the party." Then I added, lamely, "I sneaked out. But only for an hour."

"What?" asked Dad, sounding surprised.

"I'm really sorry," I said, looking away from him.

"You actually went?" asked Dad, obviously trying to get his head around the idea.

I didn't trust myself to speak, but I managed to nod. As I looked back at him, I saw disappointment flood his face.

"With Ellie?" asked Jan sharply.

I didn't want to drop Ellie in it so I'd started to say no

when I heard, "Yeah, it was all my idea. I made her come."

I spun around and saw Ellie, in her pajamas, standing in the doorway. She walked over to the table and sat down next to me.

"I'd already told everyone I was going, Mum, and then you changed your mind. I was mad. So I sneaked out. Frankie just came to keep me company."

I think I was even more shocked than Dad was. I so hadn't expected Ellie to say anything. And now she was even trying to take all the blame.

"I could've said no, Ellie," I said, not wanting it to sound like she'd made me go. "It's not your fault."

She smiled really warmly at me. And it almost made it okay, but then Dad said, in his most hurt voice, "I can't believe you'd do that, Frankie. I don't know what to say."

"Oh, please," said Ellie, sounding angry.

Jan looked at her. "Ellie," she snapped, like a warning.

"You guys keep us a secret from each other, and then drag us on vacation just so you can hang out together the whole time and pretty much ignore us. Of course we're going to sneak out and go to a party," said Ellie.

She was right. It sucked enough that Dad and Jan hadn't told us about each other, but then they left us alone most of the time. All we'd done was sneak out to a party for an hour. I felt like I had to say something, so I piped up with, "And at least we told you the truth."

Jan and Dad looked at each other. Obviously they were thinking about what we'd said.

Then Jan nodded. "Fair point, El. We should have told you about each other. And we should be doing more things all together," she said. "It wasn't the plan to leave you guys to entertain each other. I guess we're just really new to this."

Dad nodded. "Look, I'm sorry too. I want us to all get along and get to know each other. But Frankie," he said, looking at me, "there's no excuse for your behavior. You deliberately went out and did something behind my back that you knew I didn't approve of. You did the right thing by coming clean, but you're still grounded."

I nodded, expecting that. I knew there wasn't much point objecting, but it was going to make the rest of the vacation pretty ordinary.

Jan took Dad's hand. "Maybe the grounding can wait until we get home from our vacation. They did tell the truth. And it was partly our fault. What do you think?" she asked him softly.

Dad looked from me to Jan. Then back at me. "Jan's right. But when we get home you're grounded for two months."

Argh, two whole months!

I'd miss out on so many things. Parties. Sleepovers. Going to the pool with Gen. But I guess at least I still got to have a vacation.

Then Ellie asked, "Can we still have surf lessons while we're here, then?"

"We?" I asked, surprised that she wanted to come too.

"It might be fun," said Ellie, shrugging.

Dad sighed. "Jan? What do you think?"

"If they promise to be careful," said Jan, looking at Ellie and me.

Dad nodded. "All right. But on one condition: from now on, no more secrets!"

I couldn't agree more.

As Ellie and I walked back into our bedroom I thought about what Dad had said. *No more secrets.* If I was going to spend the rest of the vacation hanging out with Ellie I had to be honest with her.

"Last night, at the party, did you kiss Luke?" I blurted out.

Ellie looked at me and laughed. "What? No! We're friends. *Just* friends."

"It's just that I saw you two dancing and you seemed so …"

Ellie flopped down on my bed and pulled me down next to her. "I'm sorry, Frankie, I didn't even think. I was just trying to make Richie jealous."

And then suddenly I knew I had been right the first time. Of *course* she liked Richie. That's why I'd seen her crying. "Because he's got a girlfriend?"

Ellie nodded. "Yep. I thought they'd broken up until last night. So I went to the party hoping …"

"And then you found out they were still together and you wanted to pretend you didn't care?" I said, finishing her sentence.

Ellie smiled at me. "Wow, you really get it."

"Yeah. I do. It happened to me a few weeks back. I liked this guy, Tom Matthews, for ages and just when I thought something was going to happen, he introduced me to Jas." I made a face just thinking about it.

"It's the worst, isn't it?" asked Ellie.

I nodded. "But you know what? In a few weeks, it won't feel so bad." And as I said it, I realized it was true. It still made me sad to think about Tom, but by the time I saw him again at school, I knew it would be okay.

Then I grinned at her. "Besides, I think surfing lessons will definitely help. Nothing like falling off a board over and over to make you stop thinking about a boy."

Ellie laughed. "Who said anything about falling off? I plan to ride a wave all the way to the shore."

"Sounds good to me."

Then Ellie really surprised me by slinging her arm around my shoulder, and saying, "I'm glad you're here,

Frankie. I think we're going to have fun."

"Yeah. Me too," I said, and I really meant it.

"Come on, Frankie, we're going to be late," Ellie said as we ran down onto the beach. It was our last surfing lesson and we'd slept in.

We'd spent all week learning about safety and balance, and we'd learned how to paddle in the shallows, but we'd also spent a lot of the week falling off our boards and neither of us could really stand up yet. But this was our last day and we were determined we'd stand up and catch a wave in to shore.

We paddled out together, just a little way, and when the instructor blew his whistle, we turned around and lay waiting for the next wave. Ellie reached out her hand for mine and grabbed it.

"Here comes a wave, El," I said, getting ready.

"It's huge!" said Ellie, laughing.

As the wave rolled towards us, Ellie and I let go of

each other and grinned. We were sucked back a little, and we paddled madly against it.

"Go, go, go," yelled Ellie, as the wave started to break.

We jumped onto our knees as it rushed forward, then both stood up, screaming and whooping at each other, as we caught it all the way until our boards got bogged in the sand. We jumped up and hugged each other, and cheered so loudly I think Dad and Jan would have heard us from the house.

Frankie DOESN'T TELL HER DAD *the truth*

Chapter Five

"I don't blame Ellie for sulking," I said finally. "She's probably sick of hanging out with me." I was certainly sick of hanging out with her all the time. Especially given how she was with Luke last night.

Jan stood up. "I'm going to get her up. Maybe a swim would help."

As Jan left the kitchen, Dad rubbed my arm and said, "Nobody could be sick of hanging out with you, Frankie."

"You obviously are," I said, before I could stop myself.

Dad looked surprised. "What do you mean, honey?"

"Well, you and Jan are just together all the time and you go off and leave me and Ellie together and we don't even know each other."

"Oh, kiddo. I'm sorry. I didn't realize you felt like that. I tried to include you last night, but you didn't want to watch the DVD with us."

Now I felt really bad. He'd just reminded me that I'd sneaked out. Part of me still wanted to tell him, but I knew he'd be furious with me, and I definitely wasn't planning on doing it again. And if I hadn't been so hurt about Dad not wanting to spend time with me, maybe I wouldn't have even gone to the party.

"Dad, I don't always want to be with you *and* Jan. Sometimes I just want to be with you." There. I'd said it.

He nodded and then smiled. "Aw, that's a nice thing to hear. I'm glad you still enjoy my company. I'm sorry you've felt left out. I wanted you to get to know Jan and Ellie, but maybe I'm doing it all wrong."

"Well, not *all* wrong. But maybe a bit."

He ruffled my hair. "I'll talk to Jan. We'll make sure we have more time for both of you. Okay?"

I nodded. "Thanks, Dad."

Ellie was in the shower when I went back to the bedroom, so I lay down on my bed and picked up my book. Before I could read more than a few lines, Dad knocked on the door.

"Frankie, honey?" he called through. "There's a boy called Luke here to see you."

"What?" I asked sharply, jumping up.

"He's upstairs. Said he missed you at the party last night," said Dad.

I realized Dad was telling me the truth. Luke really was upstairs. I had no idea why, but I did know I wasn't even dressed yet. I was still in my tank top and shorts, and I had bad morning hair and disgusting breath. Nice. Ellie had locked the bathroom door so I couldn't do much about either.

"Coming!" I yelled. I threw on some clothes and tried to flatten down my bed head with my hands. It was hopeless, so I tied my hair up in a ponytail and went out.

"He seems nice," said Dad, arching an eyebrow, obviously amused by my panicked state.

I nodded, confused about why Luke was in the house and why he wanted to see me, but relieved that he hadn't blown my cover. I walked into the kitchen and I saw him leaning against the counter chatting to Jan. He had on the same clothes he'd been wearing at the party.

"Morning, Frankie," said Luke with that gorgeous grin of his.

I managed a hi.

Jan smiled at me. "Luke was just telling me about the party last night. Seems you girls missed a good one. Now that your dad has met Luke I'm sure he won't mind if you go to the next one."

Next one? I still had no idea what Luke was doing here.

"Want to come for a walk to the beach, Frankie?" asked Luke.

I looked at Dad. Would he say yes? He shrugged and then nodded.

"Okay," I said, walking over to Luke.

I wasn't used to boys I liked being around my parents, and Luke seemed way too confident about how to behave around Jan and Dad. It made me even more nervous.

We didn't say anything until we'd walked down the path away from the house, I think we both knew that Jan and Dad might have overheard. But as soon as we were out of earshot, I burst out with, "What are you doing here?"

"Glad to see me, are you?" said Luke.

"No! I mean, yes! I don't know," I said, sounding even more ditzy and confused than I felt.

"You ran off last night. You didn't even say good-bye," said Luke.

"Yeah. You were dancing with Ellie, remember? Didn't look like you cared if I was there or not," I said, sounding hurt and angry.

"Come on," he said, grabbing my hand. I let myself get pulled along through the garden, still wondering what he was doing. His hand felt so warm and soft in mine that even though I was cross and confused, I didn't want to pull away.

We walked all the way down the road to his house and neither of us said anything. I still didn't know if he'd kissed Ellie.

He led me through his house, out the back door and down the hill. It was weird being back in the same place after last night. I almost expected to see people still dancing.

We reached a set of little grassy steps that led out to a sort of platform. Luke led me to the very end. And the view was amazing. Standing on tiptoes I could peep down over the cliffs and see the beach. The sun was already super bright and the water was covered in gold light. It was beautiful.

"Wow," I said, unable to help myself.

Luke smiled at me, obviously happy that I was so impressed. "I tried to show you this last night, but it was too dark. See the waves? It's a perfect break," said Luke.

"Yeah," I said. I still had no idea what I was doing

here. This was his spot. The place he came to check out the surf. The place he'd wanted to show me at the party. Just as I was about to ask him what had happened last night with Ellie, he turned me around to face him and slid his hands around my waist, pulling me close.

"Hi," he said, his breath soft.

"Hi," I said, smiling.

Then he leaned forward and kissed me on the mouth. A soft, sweet, warm kiss that went on for ages.

We broke apart, and neither of us said anything for a while.

"Sorry, was that okay?" asked Luke.

"I'm just feeling a bit confused," I said. "When I left the party you and Ellie were together on the dance floor. I thought you two might have ..." and I trailed off because I didn't really know how to ask him whether he'd kissed Ellie.

Luke laughed. "Kissed? No way. I just kissed you, though."

"But you guys looked so close," I said, sounding a bit pathetic.

"We're friends, Frankie. It didn't mean anything. I think she was trying to make Richie jealous because she likes him, and his girlfriend was there last night. I don't know. But I'm not interested in Ellie. I'm interested in you. So can you stop ruining the moment?" he said, sounding a bit put out.

I smiled at him. He was right. Here was this gorgeous boy who had just kissed me in this amazing place and all I could do was talk about Ellie. I'd clearly lost my mind. There was plenty of time to ask Ellie what had happened. And I didn't really care anymore, anyway. Luke had just kissed me.

He went to say something, but this time it was my turn to lean forward and kiss him on the mouth. And this time it was perfect.

Frankie GETS HER EARS *pierced*

Chapter Five

"Owwwww!" I yelled, gripping Ellie's arm.

"It's not that bad," she said, as the woman checked to see if the earring had gone in correctly.

"Maybe one will do," I said, pretty happy to stop right there. If someone had warned me it was going to hurt so much, I would have been quite happy putting it off a while longer.

"It'll be over in a minute," said Ellie.

I didn't yell quite so loudly when my other ear was pierced, and Ellie was right, it was over in a minute.

After the woman had sold me a special spray to avoid any infections, Ellie dragged me away to go shopping for cool earrings. I'd have to wear the gold piercing studs for at least four weeks, but I'd be able to take them out before school started back and then I could wear some really nice ones.

As we walked down the little row of shops, I kept touching my ears to check that they were really pierced. "Thanks, Ellie," I said.

"My pleasure," she said, smiling. "Now we just have to hide your ears from your dad!"

Hmmm. My dad. I'd managed not to think about him since agreeing to get my ears pierced. He'd be cross. He might even ground me. I thought about trying to hide them from him until my birthday, but it seemed impossible. He was pretty good at working things out. Besides, it didn't feel right, keeping things from him. I'd already lied to him once in the last twenty-four hours.

Ellie took me into the shop she'd bought her earrings from. It was this tiny little place full of gorgeous things. I couldn't decide between the green and pink studs, so Ellie told me she'd buy one pair for me as an early birthday present and I could buy the other. As much as I was enjoying hanging out with her, it was a bit odd that she was being so nice to me. Was it because I covered for her when she went off to the party?

Walking back along the beach, we spotted Luke and Richie in their wetsuits and carrying their boards.

"Hey! Let's catch up with them," I said.

"No, I just want to get home," said Ellie, flicking her long blonde hair over her shoulder.

"Why?" I asked.

She shrugged. "No reason," she said.

I didn't feel like I could argue with her or chat to them on my own, so I sort of had no choice but to follow her up onto the path. But Luke must have spotted us too because he called out, "Ellie! Frankie!"

Ellie waved but made no effort to head towards them.

"What's wrong?" I asked again.

"Richie's got a girlfriend," she said. "I wanted to go to the party last night to see him. But it turns out …" she trailed off.

"Oh," I said, finally understanding. "That sucks, Ellie. I'm so sorry."

"Yeah, it does suck," she said. "Anyway, I just want to avoid him today."

I nodded. It was like what had happened with Tom, and I totally got it. Then I heard myself saying, "There's this guy I liked at school. Tom Matthews. He's so cute and I had such a huge crush on him. And it turned out …"

"Girlfriend?" Ellie arched an eyebrow at me.

"Bingo." I laughed, and Ellie laughed too. We kept walking towards home. "Let's go see how all my clothes look with my new earrings!" I suggested.

"Okay," said Ellie. "And maybe later we can get the 'rents to take us somewhere."

I forgot all about hanging out with Luke and Richie that afternoon. Right now, it seemed like Ellie needed company.

Within about three seconds of getting back to the house Dad asked, "Frankie, are they earrings?"

Ellie shot me a look.

"Yeah," I said, knowing I was in for it.

"It's not your birthday yet," he said coolly.

"I know." I knew I really didn't have much of a defense.

Jan walked into the family room and saw Dad staring at me. "Everything okay?" she asked.

Great. Now I was about to get her take on it as well. That was all I needed.

"Seems Frankie went and had her ears pierced without permission," he said to Jan.

The weird thing was, I'm pretty sure I saw Jan smile, which I didn't understand, given how tough she'd been when I left my flip-flops near the walkway last night.

"Oh," said Jan. "Ellie, do you know anything about this?" she asked.

"Yeah, it was my idea. What's the biggie? She's fourteen in two weeks," said Ellie.

Jan nodded. "You know, maybe that's the problem.

John, we have different rules for the kids and they're a bit confused about which rules count."

I was surprised. I hadn't expected Jan to be on my side. Dad must have already spoken to her and she was trying to be more understanding.

Dad shook his head. "No, Frankie knew the rule, and she ignored it."

"Yeah, you're right. I did. But I'm on vacation, and Ellie and I had fun. That's what you guys want, isn't it? For us to have fun?" I said, looking straight at Dad.

Jan walked closer to Dad. She put her hand on his arm and said quietly, "You know, John, these two girls were probably the only two kids in the whole place who didn't go to that party last night. They could have sneaked out, and they didn't."

"That's true" said Dad. "But –"

"Does it really matter if she got her ears pierced early?" asked Jan.

I waited for Dad to say something. I was expecting to be grounded anyway.

But instead he nodded. "Okay, Frankie. Looks like

you've been saved this time."

"Thanks, Jan!" I was shocked she'd gone to bat for me.

She smiled at me. A big friendly smile. And I hoped it meant that we'd get along a little better than we had been.

"And your dad and I were just talking about surfing lessons," she said, looking from him to me.

"Yeah?" I asked, my fingers crossed.

"He said you're a good swimmer," said Jan.

Ellie answered for me. "She is. She used to be on the swim team."

"You can do the lessons, Frankie," said Dad. "But no more going off and getting things pierced."

"Can I have lessons too?" asked Ellie.

I looked at her, surprised.

She shrugged in that Ellie way. "Might be fun watching you fall off a board," she said and then smiled. It reminded me of the way Luke and his sister were towards each other – teasing, but laughing at the same time.

I grinned. I couldn't believe I was getting everything I wanted. All at once. "So can I get my tongue done next?" I said to Dad.

Dad laughed. "Don't push it, kiddo."

Frankie DOESN'T GET HER EARS *pierced*

Chapter Five

"I'd better not. Mum and Dad have both said I have to wait till I'm fourteen," I explained.

Ellie rolled her eyes at me. "You already missed out on a party. You'll never have any fun if you don't do anything wrong," she said.

"I have fun," I said, like I was trying to defend myself. "Gen and I have heaps of fun."

"Well, it's a pity Gen's not here now, isn't it?" said Ellie, and she stormed out of the room.

I didn't really understand why Ellie was so angry with me. They were my ears and I'd be the one who'd get in trouble if Dad found out I went against his rules, so it was up to me. Besides, I wanted to get my ears pierced when it was a special occasion, with Mum or Gen, not with Ellie standing there and being all superior about it.

"Frankie." Dad was standing in the doorway.

"Yeah?" I asked.

"Um, is everything okay?" he said quietly.

"Not really," I said, tired of trying to pretend.

He came in and sat on the edge of my bed. "Did you and Ellie …" he sort of trailed off.

I nodded. "She wanted me to go and get my ears pierced," I said, hoping I didn't need to spell it out for him.

"Oh," he said. "And you told her you weren't allowed?"

I shrugged. I didn't really want to talk about any of this with Dad. "It's fine, Dad. Just because you and Jan are together doesn't mean Ellie and I are going to be awesome friends," I said.

"Maybe you've just been together too much," he said, and I totally agreed.

"Well, I saw in the local paper there's an old vinyl market on today. It's not far from here. Just a half-hour drive," he said with a smile. "Fancy going?"

Dad and I spent a fair bit of time searching for old vinyl. It was sort of our thing. There was just one problem. I really didn't want to go if Jan or Ellie was coming. I just wanted to go with Dad. I wasn't sure how to say that without sounding like a spoiled brat or like I was being rude about his girlfriend.

"Um," I said, pausing to try to work out what to say.

Dad nodded. He must have understood, because he said, "Just you and me, Frankie. Jan's not really into vinyl."

I couldn't help the smile that spread across my face at that news.

"Meet you at the car in five," he said.

The vinyl market wasn't as big as some we'd been to in the city. It was a little country hall with a few collectors but still Dad and I managed to spend about three hours searching through all the boxes. Dad haggled over prices and between us we came out with Neil Young's *Harvest* album, The Smiths' *The Queen Is Dead*, a Bob Dylan classic, The Velvet Underground's self-titled album, and a Blondie best-of record that I'd wanted for ages.

Then, just as we were leaving, he spotted an old record player under one of the tables. He dashed off and I saw him give the collector twenty dollars for it, and walk back to me beaming.

"Not much point buying new records if we can't listen to them," he said with a huge grin.

"Awesome," I said, laughing.

Neither of us could wait to listen to everything we bought, so we didn't bother stopping for lunch. Dad just drove the fastest way back to the house.

There was no one home when we got there, so Dad went to work hooking up the record player to Jan's stereo, and I made us some cheese sandwiches. It wasn't quite up to Ellie's food standards but it would do.

"Neil first?" asked Dad, not waiting for an answer.

We sat down on the floor, sandwiches on our laps, and waited for the crackle of the record to start. The sound was pretty good, given how tatty the record player was.

And that was where Jan and Ellie found us when they walked in with giant paper packages of fish-and-chips. We were lying on the floor, our eyes closed, just listening to "Heart of Gold."

"Is that Neil Young?" asked Jan. Dad tried to shush her, but I looked up and gave her a nod.

"I love this song," she said, sitting down on the floor near Dad.

"I've never heard of it. Sounds like old people's music," said Ellie with a cheeky grin.

Dad pretended to glare.

Ellie sat down next to me on the floor. "Happy early birthday," she whispered, handing me a tiny package. I unwrapped the paper, and inside was a pair of earrings just like the ones Ellie was wearing but green.

"Wow! Thanks, Ellie. They're beautiful," I said, surprised. I'd been thinking she was still put out that I wouldn't get my ears pierced, so it was doubly special getting a present. It meant she understood.

She smiled at me. "Thought green was your color."

"Yeah, they're perfect," I said, smiling back.

Jan opened the packages of fish-and-chips and put them between us so we could sit around on the floor, having a picnic and licking the salt off our fingers.

As we ate and argued about which records we wanted to listen to, I realized it was the first time we'd all been together when it wasn't weird. Nobody was feeling upset or mad, no one was jealous or uncomfortable. We were all just being normal. Like a family. And it felt good.

Can't get enough of
Choose Your Own Ever After?

Here is a sneak peek of

HOW TO *Get To Rio*

"Cam-ping." I said the word like I'd just discovered new vocab. "What, like, in an actual tent?"

Izzy rolled her eyes. "Of course," she said. "So, what do you say?"

"It'll be totally fun," Mia gushed.

I wasn't so sure about that. "But wasn't the last time you went camping the worst week of your lives?" I asked them. "Didn't you say it rained the whole time? And didn't one of your brothers throw up all over your sleeping bags?"

"Come on, Kitty," Izzy said, yanking her math book out of her locker. "What else will you be doing?"

Nothing. That was the problem. It was the last week of school and come next week Mum and Dad would be working, so I'd be stuck at home the entire vacation. That would be fine if I had someone to hang out with. But all my friends were going away, which left me alone with my little sister and her gang of dweebs.

I shrugged. "Okay, I'll come." I knew Mum and Dad would let me go. Izzy and Mia grinned and leaned in for a group hug. "That's provided I survive first period. I haven't done my geography assignment for Blackmore."

"I promise, we'll have *so* much fun," Mia squealed.

"Good luck with your assignment," said Izzy.

I watched them rush off to their homeroom class, their ponytails, wet from water polo practice that morning, dripping down their backs. Izzy and Mia looked like twins from behind. In fact, they looked pretty similar from the front as well. Their homeroom teacher called them both *Mizzy* because he couldn't tell them apart.

I turned back to my locker, frowning. I loved Izzy and Mia to bits. I'd known them since preschool, and they were definitely my best friends. So of course I wanted to go on vacation with them. But camping?

The only tent I'd ever slept in was the fairy princess one that Mum bought when I was three. And that tent was pitched in my room, not in the actual bush.

Mia's and Izzy's families were outdoors addicts and had been camping together heaps of times. But sleeping on the ground was not my idea of fun. Not to mention the spiders, snakes and whatever else that would be trying to get into my sleeping bag with me. Add to that communal bathrooms and long hikes in the bush. Nope. "Fun" was not the word that came to mind. But what choice did I have if I wanted to spend time with my best friends?

I grabbed my geography books out of my locker and spun around, almost crashing straight into Persephone. I got a great big whiff of her perfume and a close-up view of her pearl earring.

I was pretty certain Persephone's vacation plans wouldn't include pitching a tent and fighting for a share of baked beans. It'd be a five-star resort for her, no doubt.

"Hey," I said, smiling.

"Hi, Kitty." Persephone rattled her combination lock and banged open her locker. "Hold on a sec. I'll walk with you."

I waited, feeling slightly confused. Persephone and I weren't exactly friends. We were in the same homeroom class, and sometimes sat together in geography and art, but we never hung out. Then I remembered how recently she'd saved me a seat a couple of times. But still, that wasn't like hanging out. And she'd never walked with me to class before. She always walked with her own friends – the cool group.

I looked around for them. "You're not waiting for –?"

"Nah," Persephone said quickly.

As we headed to class, I was feeling a bit stunned to be walking with one of the coolest girls in our year ...

What will happen next? Has Kitty just made a cool new friend? Will she go camping with Mia and Izzy? Find out in *How To Get To Rio!*

Choose Your Own Ever After ... the series where YOU get to make the decisions, and choose where the story goes. Follow your heart right to the end or go back and choose all over again!